vc 1-10
9

SFM

RIDERS IN THE DUSK

Lige Wyatt's father Henry had found a solution to starving out on his homestead—he sold fresh, strong horses to fugitive outlaws. He did well at it—until the day four strangers, federal lawmen, appeared. Then one of the outlaws Henry Wyatt had outfitted raided the nearby town of Lincoln, and an irate posse of local men rode up to lynch Henry and Lige. Surprisingly, the plans of the lawmen and those of the possemen didn't seem to coincide . . . When it was all over, no one in Lincoln liked what the lawmen had done, and the lawmen did not give a damn: they were satisfied that what they had done was right—not legal, but right . . .

RIDERS
IN THE DUSK

Frank Bosworth

A Lythway Book

CHIVERS PRESS
BATH

First published in Great Britain 1974
by
Robert Hale Limited
This Large Print edition published by
Chivers Press
by arrangement with
Robert Hale Limited
1986

ISBN 0 7451 0290 5

© Robert Hale Limited 1974 and 1982

British Library Cataloguing in Publication Data

Bosworth, Frank
  Riders in the dusk.—Large print ed.—
  (A Lythway book)
  Rn: Lauran Paine   I. Title
  813'.54[F]   PS3566.A34

  ISBN 0–7451–0290–5

RIDERS IN THE DUSK

CHAPTER ONE

THE WATCHER

He stood barefooted in the warm, dark earth where the ploughshare had turned up great rolls of virgin sod, watching the sun teeter upon a faraway hog-backed ridge, its immense rays spreading flames of blood and copper, inundating all the world for one last blazing moment.

Then the blue shadows came, like a veil of mist, falling gently upon the nearer hills, and the sun died, skewered by a pinnacle, so that the blue-veiled shadows could spread and thicken, creep down from those distant mountains, dip as low as the swales, mount up over the nearer hills and come tumbling down towards him, where he kept the vigil in the fresh-ploughed earth out a hundred yards and more from the log cabin, the log barn, the peeled-log corrals, all tucked in a remote place, but for all that, squatting clear of the westerly forest because, as the watcher's father had said often enough, his folks died because they built with their backs to a forest, and there had been others, back in Missouri who'd done the same foolish thing. It could have been Indians; folks had told his father that was who killed his parents, but now,

1

so many years later, his father would take a deep swallow from the crockery jug and shake his head, then he'd say, 'No In'ians done that. No sir. No In'ians. But I wasn't a whole lot older'n you in them days, so I believed it. Only I'm a lot older now. I know how renegades leave a mark. In'ians like hell; it was renegades. Probably Jayhawkers, maybe some of those marauding Texans. We always had them Texans to look out for when I was your age, Lige.'

Maybe it was the Texans, and maybe it had been the Indians. Lige had never known any of his grandparents, so it probably didn't matter a whole lot. Except that he winced from the thought of death.

The dusk settled in, but this time of year— summer—it took it a long while to get settled in, and meanwhile the boy stood as still as stone, moving only his sharp, wary grey eyes. He had learned long ago that most creatures only see movement; in places where they don't expect to see anything, if a body stands plumb still even a mounted man can ride within a hundred feet or so, and never notice anything, providing there's some kind of background to darken it where a body stands.

There was no background out where his father had done the ploughing, but there was the oncoming evening, and that would be just as good.

He had no idea how long he'd have to stand

there. Nor did it matter. When his father said stand and watch, Lige knew better than to depart even so much as a fraction from those instructions.

Over where the creek ran, some berry bushes looked black, but a new-growth stand of poplars and cottonwoods still showed pale green leaves. There was another tree, the watcher had never known its name, and now it still showed maize yellow in spite of the shadows. His mother was buried a hundred paces this side of that maize-yellow tree. She'd wanted to be buried directly beneath it, but afterwards his father said that if the creek rose ... so they had put her down a hundred paces inland. His father had hauled a great flat stone from up-country somewhere, and had chiselled her name and the date of her passing upon it, then he had imbedded the big stone flush with the ground, in a nest of creekgravel.

They made out. His father had said they would, and they were doing it. But sometimes it was very hard to eat supper off the old pewter plates that had been his mother's treasure; she'd lugged them in crates plumb across from Council Bluffs in their wagon. She'd also had a fine lavender dress and a real tortoise-shell comb, but she'd been buried with them, so all that was left was the pewter. Sometimes he could almost hear her washing them in the wooden tub out back after supper; hear her

3

sluicing off the pewter plates, and occasionally coughing.

Something moved against the deeper black of the forested uplands, which were many miles distant, something that was lighter than the shadows and lighter than the dusk. The boy stood very still tracing out that stealthy soft and silent movement without looking directly at it. He looked inches *beyond* it, which was the way to see things best at night.

It was a rider. That was all he had to know. He stood, straining to run back, until the rider passed down the far side of a low, grassy hillock, then the boy turned and sped with the grace of a blue-doe all the way to the cabin, where his father, a thick, powerful, but not overly tall man was sitting upon a tipped-back chair he'd made, smoking his pipe with the crockery jug beside him upon the hard-packed earth. He looked up when the lad came on soundless feet.

'Rider's coming,' gasped the boy.

'How far out?'

'Not far. Can't see very far this late at night. Maybe half mile.'

His father arose, picked up the jug and stepped inside. When the boy also entered the cabin and instinctively moved towards a lamp— it was his job to light them at evening—his father growled at him.

'Leave it be, Lige. No lights. You go watch out back. If you see him, thump on the wall and

4

I'll hear you. I'll keep watch this side. I kind of don't think he'll come riding straight in, though. Not this one.'

Lige looked up, his curly, thick mane of russet hair half tumbled across his forehead. 'Who is he; who is the man out there?'

'Boy, just do like you're told and don't forever be asking questions. Now scat around the far side and keep your eyes skinned. Just remember—thump the logs and I'll hear.'

The dusk hung on. It always brought a dead-like hush this time of year. In early springtime pheasants drummed and quail called, and mourning doves sailed in at dusk to make their wonderfully soft-sad sound as they perched along the creek-bank high up. But in full summer the dusk was a still, drowsy time. The best thing to hear now was the snuffling of horses in the barn, or beyond it, out among the corrals, and sometimes a cow calling her calf before darkness settled and the wolves roamed. But there hadn't been any wolves around the past couple of years. At least not in daytime.

Lige was a dead shot and so was his father. The last wolf that had skulked in too close had been rolled end over by his father's .45–.70. Wolves were smart animals, nigh as smart as a man, at times. Foxes and coyotes were also smart.

Lige went to his own bedroom, which was small but weatherproof, and knelt by a rear

5

window, watching. There was no glass of course, only thick wooden shutters which bolted from the inside with steel thole pins. To get inside the cabin of Henry Wyatt a man would need a very sharp axe, a stout crowbar, and a lot of muscle. Also, after the first blow, he'd need a miracle to remain alive.

The cabin had four rooms and a lean-to. It was low-ceilinged and fort-like. The logs had come at great labour from those far-away mountains to the north and west. The cabin had been two years in the building, but that was mainly because Henry Wyatt had to do other things to keep his wife and son fed and warm. A hard-pressed man, Henry Wyatt, he had never shirked work because he'd never been able to afford to do that. Not in all his life.

Lige kept kneeling and peering, but by now it was so dark around the barn and the cabin that unless the rider in the dusk came almost up to the log-wall, he could not be seen very easily. If he came up, then stood stock-still, he couldn't be seen at all.

Lige hunkered and watched, and wondered. He had no fear of them, really, and this wasn't the first one by a long shot. His father always made out like it was something dangerous and mysterious, and Lige knew better because twice now, he'd snuck out back of the barn when his father had met them, had taken their money, had made arrangements, then had given them

6

their pick of the corraled animals, and they had gone on again.

A hard-pressed man, Henry Wyatt. He'd had to do many things on the frontier to keep food and warmth close by his family.

Lige closed his eyes then sprang them wide again—and saw fluid motion out just a short distance from the cabin. He balled a fist and commenced knocking upon the logs.

An owl called, the moon glided behind a thick cloud, the world turned darker and seemed to end just ten feet from the boy's window. Another owl answered.

Lige did not abandon his vigil, but he slackened it and let his eyes, like his thoughts, wander. There was no more need to keep watch. Not after that second owlhoot.

He was hungry, too. His father had sent him to the ploughed ground just as he'd been coming from choring at the barn. His mother had never done this, but then women were very different from men.

But hunger, although it was no respecter of meals if it was prolonged enough, happened to also be a great stimulator of recollection. He hunkered and thought back; his mother had been able to make pone so crusty and light and golden. For something special she'd poured 'lasses upon it. She'd been able to stir up kidney beans, blanched corn-kernels and brown sugar into a meal fit for the President. Once, during

7

their first winter, though, she'd gathered acorns from the red and white oaks to make sourbread, and Lige had helped by tending the leaching fires. That winter they'd had a cow; she had more-likely kept them all from dying with her butter and sweetmilk, and cheese and clabber and curds. The very next summer the cow disappeared. His father always maintained those big, rich cowmen to the north and east had stolen her by moonlight, but Lige could not reconcile this, with how the cowmen and their hired riders scorned soddy-people, log-hut people who raised patches of cabbage and suchlike, and kept cows to milk. Cattlemen not only didn't drink milk, but they were contemptuous of both milk cows and the people who brought them to the range country.

If cowmen had indeed stolen their cow, why then more-likely they had run her to some canyon-rim somewhere, shot her and tumbled her to the depths.

They were worse than the In'ians, Lige knew for a fact. His father told him so. He'd also heard it from the other homesteaders down lower where the richer ground was, nearer the cowtown of Lincoln, which was named for the man who had been U.S. President when Lige's father had been a boy.

CHAPTER TWO

THE WAY LIFE IS

Every man had to live with inherent contradictions. Henry Wyatt, built like a two-year old bull, thick and oaken and massive, but not overly tall, had all his life despised liars, and yet he led a life which was two-thirds of a lie from dawn until dusk. He farmed his upland trough-farm between the soft, bald hills, and he had accumulated a few cattle which he allowed the run of the free-graze, but that was not, in truth, how he made his living.

Another thing that men did, if they remained long enough in one place, they reached some kind of accommodation with the depth of their soil; if it was good, rich land and there was plenty of it, they became comfortable and secure living atop it, but if, as with Henry Wyatt, they hadn't 'taken up' good land, or not enough of it, why then they ultimately came down to the level of their land; if it was poor, they became poor; if it was distant and isolated, they became that way too.

And if their homestead was athwart a route from north to south, from the empty mountains north and west to the open country leading down across Colorado from Wyoming into New

Mexico and all the Border Country beyond Raton Pass, then sooner or later they saw the shadowy riders pass, and without knowing precisely why those silhouettes crossed their land in the silent dusk, they could piece together enough of it to understand that their homestead was on the historic outlaw-trail. They adapted to that, as well.

Even if they refused to discuss it, because, as with oaken Henry Wyatt, they did not believe in liars or in lying. Evidently a man could live a lie, if he never talked of it.

The morning after that rider in the dusk had come and gone, Lige ate porridge in the lean-to kitchen with his father, without either of them saying a word. This was, for them both, always the worst time; after the outlaw had come, had whispered down by the barn in darkness, had passed over money and had taken the fresh horse. Give it a few days, and things between father and son became easy again. Except for memory. But Lige had been snarled into silence often enough for his curiosity, to keep memory to himself.

Once, a year back, a party of expressionless horsemen had walked their horses into the yard from down at Lincoln. They had looked at the horses in the barn and out back in the corrals, and they had sat an hour or so in quiet conversation with Henry Wyatt. Lige had seen them from over by the creek where he'd taken the worn-out and head-hung horse of the man who had passed the previous night, to let the animal graze out of sight of the cabin. The strangers had got astride, eventually, and had gone back down-country.

All Henry had told his son was that an outlaw had struck in Lincoln just before dawn, had killed two men in a robbery, and had himself been killed, and someone had said he was certain the outlaw's fresh horse had been up there in that immigrant's corrals only a couple of days earlier.

Henry never told his son that he had lied, had said that he had indeed owned that claybank gelding, and he'd been fixing to come to town to report the theft that same day.

Otherwise, not very many people visited the uplands where the Wyatt place was. Before his mother had died, some of the other immigrants had driven up, some Sundays, in their old wagons, and everyone had eaten and laughed and had pitched horseshoes until late afternoon. But for the past several years those people rarely ever came near any more. Lige wished they would. His father always said the same thing, 'It's hard, son; Wyoming's worse than the middle states for snow and cold. Folks got to get in their crops and got to tend things all summer, just to put down enough to eat through the winters. They'll come, don't you fret about that. It's just that we're a long way up here, and folks

11

got so much to do when they make a new life.'

Maybe. But they never came, and after three years it seemed that surely *some* of them anyway, ought to be able to scare up the time. One Sunday out of a summer of Sundays wasn't so terribly much.

Once, some bedraggled redskins came straggling on a diagonal, aimless course from the mountains. They had traded pemmican and four young horses for two gallons of corn squeezings from Henry Wyatt's private stock of whisky, which was kept in the dark coolness of the well-house, then they had gone on and Henry had pointed after them. 'You see; whenever a man figures he's got to the bottom and can't go no lower, he runs across something like *them*. I remember a big 'breed buck up on Green River one time. He'd been to school and he told me his people were the lords of the north plains. When he told me that he was so sodden drunk he could hardly stand up. There go the lords of the north plains, and now we'd best go see what we can make of them colts.'

Henry Wyatt always had sleek horses. He did not steal them; no shrewd man ever stole horses, only fools did that. The head-hung, ridden-down and wrung-out horses he got in trade from the duskriders—at least eight out of ten of them—he could bring back. Mostly, all they needed was lots of rest, plenty of rich feed, and maybe a little doctoring for saddle- or cinch-sores.

He seldom bought a horse. A man with his back to the wall learns the same way a weasel or a wolf or a rock-chuck learns. If he *hadn't* learned, he would have starved out long ago.

The outlaws bought his sleek animals and they didn't actually trade him their animals, although he always made them think that was what they were doing. He'd jack-up the price of one of his good animals in direct proportion to the poor condition of the outlaw's animal, then he'd call it a 'trade' with the result that the outlaw *bought* Henry Wyatt's animal, and gave Henry *his* animal. There was nothing wrong with that; horsetraders had been growing rich doing that since time out of mind.

Lige learned much from his father. He already knew how to gain a horse's confidence. He had learned how to mud-pack bowed tendons, how to heal closed bullet grazes and bear-claw tears with alum and powdered blue vitriol, and powdered sulphur. He knew how to salve kidney sores and cinch-sores that looked like raw meat. He could ride mean ones and gentle the half-wild ones.

There was always enough to do. More than enough, in fact, to keep his mind off that other thing—the thing he and his father did not talk about, although they could talk well on any other subject.

He worked at the seeding too, side by side

with his father, which was not difficult since Lige was already, at sixteen, three inches taller, even if he didn't weigh within thirty or forty pounds of the older man. They would put on the broadcasting sacks made of old blanketing, with the leather harness-strap slung around from under the right side up and around the neck and down to the left side, holding the sack with its fifty-pound weight of barley, oat and wheat seed, then they would walk upon the warm, yielding dark earth, which was their seedbed, and with rhythmic sweeps, send forth the golden fruit of last year's threshing. Before the crows could get it all, they would then drive the horses back and forth to trample in the seed, and afterwards, they would sit of an evening watching hopefully for the first wet clouds to soar slowly down-country from the north. All the best growing rains came from the north. Sometimes, too, the north sent them late frosts. If that happened three days running, it would very often kill the crop; the barley and oats— always the oats—but that left the wheat.

They had made the adjustment to this new country. The year Lige's mother had been taken off, was the first time his father had been able to take his wife and son to Lincoln and buy the boy a sack of rock-candy, and buy his wife gingham dress-goods. If she had stayed with them another three years . . .

But she hadn't been able to do that.

The summer had not been long over the land. This was evident, for, over along the creek where Lige spent as much time as he dared, because it was sweet-smelling and cool, and someway or another, it drew him to it and held him in its peace; over there new shoots still stood pale in the loam, soft leaves without their full colour were upon the new tree limbs.

Summer was a golden time, until late, then it became hot by night as well as by day, but that did not last long. Frost could come any time after August. Not usually, of course, but Lige had seen it come as early as the second week in September. Wyoming's high country, as Henry Wyatt had often said, did not have a good growing season; it was too short.

But it was good cow-country; at least the buffalo grass which never grew tall nor lush, had an extraordinary strength to it. Cattle that lived through a winter got fat from the inside out, in sometimes only a month or two. Lately, there was talk of sheep coming too, but around Lincoln the stockmen scoffed. Too many wolves, they said, too many coyotes and panthers and bears. And also they said, too many guns.

There *were* sheep, but not in the high-plateau country. Lige's father shook his head. 'They'll never dast come this far north. Cowmen've had this country too long. Look what they done for a while against homesteaders, until the army put a

15

stop to it, and mostly, they didn't really fear squatters, they just didn't like them. But maybe a thousand sheep in a band, maybe five thousand . . . They wouldn't last a month.'

No one was concerned. Wyoming was cow-country from the Yellowstone to the Cache Le Poudre, and cattle had been good for Wyoming. So good, in fact, that the Territory had been sounding like a State, every town had a bank, the stages ran to schedule, dignitaries even from the far Potomac around Washington, occasionally came out to Wyoming, there were mines too, and growing numbers of people, and wealth—and outlaws in proportion.

There was also the vacuum Lige existed in. Where the Indians had left a hunting preserve, along with their pony-trails, their tipi-rings, their raggedy old dessicated corpses lashed high in the trees, now there was just the vacuum. Lige inherited a lot of this, as much of it as he could roam over between choretimes, to hunt and fish, and without his father realizing it, Lige was digesting much that the Indians had abandoned. He could stalk soundlessly, he could catch light and shadow and movement through pre-dawn and post-dusk. He could track and scent and ambush. No one taught him; no one taught anyone who ever lived close to the world of earth-clouds and prairie-mountains; people adapted and if they were young, they did it better and faster.

Like the rusty dawn with an overcast sky when Lige went out as he always had to do early, and stood just for a moment on the lee-side of the outhouse sounding the new-wrought day, and felt an alien presence. It was something that came down to him from his natural world, like a telegraph signal; something was there that did not belong there. He stood stone-still and waited until the movement came, low to the ground, cautious and supple. Not, he felt, the kind of movement anything with two legs could make. He waited longer, then turned back to the house and roused his father.

Henry got the .45–.70 and knelt by a front window.

But the sun came, the animals complained about not being fed on time, and Lige went forth, finally, his father behind him giving gun-cover, to do his chores.

They did not see it again, although Henry did not question his son, and Lige knew very well it had been out there.

'Panther,' suggested Henry Wyatt. 'In late calving season they come, like the coyotes, sometimes, to the calving grounds for whatever they can glean.'

That afternoon, though, at the creek in among the willows, Lige saw the flat-heeled boot-track. It went down to the water. There were two smudges which would be knee-marks, and a perfect imprint of a steel butt-plate, then

17

the tracks went down through the undergrowth and lost themselves because someone wanted them to get lost.

Lige went back to the barn where his father was shoeing, and related what he had seen. Henry Wyatt was not upset. He listened, then he said, 'Well; some hunter more-likely, son.'

And that night Lige was sent out to keep vigil again, and later he was also sent to his room to watch from there. Meanwhile, his father, who was supposedly out front in the parlour, had slipped on silent feet out back of the barn to meet someone with a honed-down horse and crisp new money.

CHAPTER THREE

A STRANGER IN THE MIST

The seed was in and the rains came, as warm and soft as a woman's tears. Afterwards, a lost cloud fell into a trough of hills westerly a few miles, and while Henry Wyatt was at work upon the copper coils of his whisky-still, Lige took his rifle and rode out where that lost cloud, unable to become airborne again, would disintegrate and die and meld with the water-warmed earth.

They had two barrels of meat salted and put down, but there was always a need for meat to jerk. But even so, for Lige, hunting was nothing he could not postpone if there was something more interesting at hand.

He reached the nearest bald hillock, rode up it and sat, gazing a hundred or so yards ahead at the fallen cloud, which was an eerie thing, like a fallen goose or an earthbound eagle; some things did not belong upon the ground and rarely seemed to come there. He had never seen an entire cloud, round and formed and perfectly cloud-shaped, lying helpless and still upon the ground.

Above, was a winey-clear sky. Everything, even the farthest mountaintops, was as clear as glass. The rain did that, washed the world and left the air dustfree with perfectly visibility.

Lige pushed the horse on down off the hillock and up into the first fog-clammy perimeter of cloud form. He rode right up on to the man before he even saw him. But the man was standing motionless, watching, his carbine hooked through a curled arm, his stiff-brimmed hat tipped up, colourless in that veil of diaphon, like a stripling tree or a pinnacle-stone.

For Lige, it was a reversed-encounter in this countryside that he prowled and knew, and overlorded among the other natural things; *he* had been caught moving, and the stranger had stood stock-still, Indian-like, to let Lige get up close enough for the horse to catch the man's gamey scent. But by then Lige had seen the shadow-form and was hauling back.

The man had weathered skin and crinkles up around dark, motionless eyes. He also had a little flare of grey at the temples but right at the moment of their meeting, Lige noticed only the stance, the ivory-handled, hip-holstered Colt, and the Winchester saddlegun draped over a bent arm.

He scarcely breathed.

The man finished his appraisal and said, 'If you saw any deer in this fog, boy, you'd never get a shot. They'd hear you before you saw them, and they'd be high-tailing it, so all you'd see would be their flags.'

The man loosened a little, studied Lige's sleek horse, then grounded his carbine and leaned a little.

'You live down yonder at the log-place?'

Lige nodded, waiting for his voice to return.

'Well now,' said the man, not unkindly, 'I've been wondering—would that be the homestead of a man named Wyatt?'

Lige's throat relaxed enough to allow an answer to form. 'Yes, sir. Henry Wyatt's my father.'

The dark eyes took on a liquid amiability. 'I wondered if maybe it wasn't. But you see, son, I don't want to just crowd up on anyone.'

Lige remembered the flat-heeled imprints and looked. Sure enough, this one had them. Mostly, riders left smaller bootheel imprints, because most rangemen wore undershot cowboy-heels. You could tell a lot about a man from his boots and hat, and other things as well. This man was not from Montana. He probably wasn't even from Wyoming or Idaho or Colorado. He was dressed more like a desert-rangeman, where the Mex—Spanish—imprint was on, not just the attire, but also upon the horsegear. But if he was a desert-man, then he was a long way from home.

'You've been around a spell,' Lige said. 'I saw your boot-tracks at the creek a few days back, along with the sign of your butt-plate.'

The man smiled, and showed strong, white teeth. 'How old are you?' he asked, and when Lige told him, he seemed pleased. 'That's a good age, and you've got enough learning to get along. What's your name?'

'Lige. Well; Elijah. My mother gave it to me—from the Good Book.'

The stranger nodded gently over that. 'Mothers always want sons to remember what's best, and to turn out that way. Is your mother down there too?'

'No sir. She died.'

The lean, sinewy man pondered that a moment. 'It's bad for women, this far from the States, Lige. It's hard on them—and horses. Now I wonder if you'd do something for me?' The stranger dipped into a trouser-pocket and brought forth a large silver coin. He held it up, then stepped close and handed it up. 'Ride down and tell your paw I'd admire to see him up here, directly. No killing hurry, but before the cloud lifts. Will you do that?'

'Yes sir. You could wait until dusk and come down to the back of the barn.'

The stranger's eyes held a depth of thought after that remark, then he shook his head. 'I reckon a lad with sense like yours doesn't miss out on much does he? No; I'd like him to come up here. I'll wait—and keep watch from that hillock you rode up onto.'

Lige turned back, clutching the silver dollar—a cartwheel—more money in cash than he had ever owned before. He thought of a red shirt he had seen last year in Lincoln. He also thought of a pair of spurs, maybe, or a hat like the stranger wore, with its intricately-worked wrought-silver buckle, keeper, and tip, which was Southwestern attire. In the far north country men wore Indian-plaited horsehair bands, mostly, or sometimes braided rawhide hatbands.

He did not think, even once, even after he had returned to the yard and was heading for the barn, that without meaning to do it, he had inadvertently ridden right into the middle of his father's secret trade with outlaws. What brought that home to him was when he met his father in the barn and told him about the stranger; that the stranger had known his father's name.

Henry Wyatt gazed steadily at his son for a moment, his face darkening with the tell-tale signs. *Then*, Lige became aware, but by then it was too late, and even if it hadn't been too late, he still would have had to tell, because otherwise the stranger surely would come to the back of the barn and hoot like an owl, so his father would have found out anyway.

Henry Wyatt had been working on their old wagon, with two wheels off and the grease bucket with its wooden paddle, close by. He straightened up and began slowly drying his hands, avoiding looking at the boy. Eventually, as he peered beyond the doorless big front opening, he said, 'Maybe he's just lost, out there. Did you see his horse?'

'No. He was just standing there. I rode right up on to him, paw. I didn't even see him until we weren't more'n fifty feet apart.'

'You'd ought to be keeping a better watch,' grumbled Henry Wyatt, and went to the peg where his hat and gunbelt hung. 'Well; whoever he is I'll go and talk to him. You can finish packing the boxings on the wagon. Never can tell when we'll need it.'

His father turned his back and brought forth a sorrel horse with small eyes and a Roman nose. It was a big, powerful beast with a blotched brand upon its left shoulder, but the first time Lige had seen it, the Roman-nosed sorrel had looked skin and bones and hadn't been able to

23

step over a small deadfall tree. That was last autumn.

Henry Wyatt's only comment about the sorrel horse had been to say, 'Idaho animal.' How he knew those things was a plumb mystery, but he knew them.

After his father had rigged out and ridden away, Lige offsaddled his own mount, turned it into a corral, put his saddlebooted carbine in a corner, and went over to finish the wheel-packing.

In three or four years, this was the first time he'd ever talked to one of those men. It was also the closest he'd ever been to one, and since this was early morning, not early evening, there had to be something uniquely different, aside from the boots and hat, and the silver trimmings, to this one.

He finished packing the wheels, jockeyed both rear wheels back up on to their spindles, then used the wheel-wrench to turn down the lugs, which turned backwards from the direction in which the wheels turned.

It was not yet quite noon, but the day had started very early, so Lige went to the cabin for bread and cold meat and well-water. When his mother had been alive there had usually been something special, sometimes something sweet, under the tin lid upon the kitchen shelf near the cast iron stove. There had been nothing under that lid now for so long Lige hardly even looked

24

at it any more.

He did not expect his father back soon. In fact, when his father rode out alone, he never tried to anticipate his return. Sometimes, his father would be gone overnight. Not very often, though. Usually, he would return by evening.

Today was different. In fact, when Lige had time to reflect back some time later, he recognized that this day was different from just about any other day in his life.

Henry Wyatt returned to the cabin, tied the big sorrel out front to the hitch-rack, stamped inside without a glance or a word even though he passed within fifteen inches of his son, then Lige heard him cursing under his breath in the bedroom his father and mother had shared. When his father stamped back through again, he still did not look at the boy. He was carrying their carpet-bag medical chest.

Lige watched him get back astride, wheel and lope back the way he had come. When it was safe to do so, the boy stepped out upon the packed-earth porch and looked in the direction of the fallen cloud. It was still out there, in the middle distance, but now it was beginning to dilute, to weaken and lose form and foggily disintegrate, probably because the sun was burning through the last of the rainclouds.

For Lige, with his sombre thoughts, what had occurred up to this point was clear enough. Since his father hadn't been injured, and since that stranger with the ivory-butted Colt hadn't looked injured, why then there had to be someone else over there in the cloudbank, who *was* injured, and that meant a third person.

Maybe it had happened before, but not that Lige knew of. One thing he *did* know, though, was that look of bleak, harsh, almost violent, disapproval on his father's face. He had seen it before, enough times.

Eventually, with the day getting along, Lige went out to look at the farmed ground. Not that he really expected to see any pale new shoots; it had only rained the day before and last night, but sometimes, when the earth was warm long enough ahead of a rain, it didn't take any more than one soft rain to bring the sprouts.

But there weren't any. Tomorrow, probably. He turned to go in the direction of the barn and saw his father coming, far out, small but recognizable on that big stout, Roman-nosed gelding. His father had the carpet-bag slung from the horn and was riding slumped as though he were troubled or lost in thought, or maybe just plain tired.

There were chores to be done before sunset. Lige could always keep busy. He re-filled the bucket for their kitchen, from the well-house, then he went down to see about pitching feed to the horses, and to the west a half mile or so, some of their cows were visible, but that was about as close as they'd come to the ranch this time of year. Only when they were hungry for days on end in mid-winter, would they overcome their fear of men and come right out back of the barn and bawl.

His father rode slowly; now and then Lige would peer out to see. Finally now, that fallen little cloud was entirely gone. Over where it had been, were some pines and firs, and even some oaks, which did not ever seem to grow at a very high elevation, as in the distant bristly-forested mountains.

His father entered the yard, turned into the barn, swung down and handed Lige the carpet-bag. 'Put it back,' he ordered detachedly, and turned to yank loose his latigo. 'And son, put your ticking in the kitchen. You'll have to bed down there for a few days.'

Lige stood still.

Henry turned, considered his son, then said, 'There's a shot-man over there. We got to help him for a spell, until he can ride again.' Henry kept looking at his son, his face loose, almost tired-looking. 'I guess you'd figure... Nothing. Just do like I say.'

Lige did. He'd always obeyed well.

CHAPTER FOUR

A BRACE OF STRANGERS

Henry Wyatt would have given almost anything if those outlaws had gone on. He'd have *given* them horses, no trade, no sale, just *given* them two fresh animals if they just hadn't stopped over there in the grassy swale.

But of course one of them couldn't have ridden on. Lige did not see this one until noon the following day, when his father came out of the bedroom—Lige's room—grey in the face. The other man, the lean, sinewy, rather handsome man with the ivory-butted Colt, had been in there too. As he passed Lige he said, 'If you had a pitcher of cold water, boy . . .'

Lige got the water, with a glass, and took them into the room.

The man lying shrivelled and lifeless upon Lige's bed was also tanned and lean and weathered-looking, as though he too had been a rangeman most of his life, living free. He could have been either younger or older than his pardner. Just looking at him, it was impossible to tell, especially now when his slack-hung lips were bluish, and his cheeks were sunken, and there were rain-like transparent beads of sweat standing upon his upper lip and forehead. He

28

could have been almost any age.

Lige filled the glass and leaned down. The man's eyelids parted as though their weight was enormous. Two very intently blue eyes looked upwards with only a very faint semblance of rationality. They remained upon Lige. The man was strong-willed, even as weak and wrung-out as he was, he did not draw inward the way dying people often did, did not begin the process of relinquishing, of turning away from things that had been very important, and which now not only weren't the least bit important, but which were ridiculous, pointless, wholly pointless.

He whispered in a husky, laboured way. 'Lift my head, boy. Hold me up . . . the water.'

Lige tried to be gentle. He also tried not to spill the chilled well-water upon the man's soggy, blood-stiffening shirtfront. He concentrated so hard upon these things he forgot to think what he was doing. He had never seen a shot-man before, and certainly never one as torn and bloody as this man was.

The water went down slowly, but it went down to the last drop. The man had been terribly thirsty. He seemed revived by the water because as Lige lowered him, he said, 'Another glass, boy . . . if you please.'

The man was hot to the touch, which meant he was burning with fever. Lige gave him only half a glass the second time, then he stayed to do for the man what he remembered his mother doing for him when he'd had swamp-complaint that bad first year on the claim; he soaked one of the rags, left behind by his father and the other man, in cold water, wiped the stranger's face clean with it, then he placed it across the man's forehead.

The intently blue eyes watched, then closed again as though the weight of the eyelids was overpowering. Lige straightened back.

'Stay,' the man said. His tongue made a clumsy circuit of fever parched lips. 'Where's Harrow . . . ?'

Harrow could only be the other stranger. 'In the kitchen,' replied Lige. 'I'll fetch him.'

'No. Boy, keep the cloth cold. Can you do that?'

'Yes sir.'

'. . . What's your name?'

'Lige Wyatt. Elijah Wyatt.'

'Lige; anyone else around, besides you'n Harrow, and the other . . . feller?'

'No sir. The other feller's my paw.'

For ten or fifteen seconds the stranger lay shallowly breathing, then he roused himself enough to say, 'All right; fetch Harrow.'

Lige went soundlessly to the kitchen where his father and the other stranger were drinking coffee. The whisky crock was on the floor beside his father's chair. The men looked up when Lige came into the room and gave his message.

'He wants to see you, mister.'

Without a word the stranger arose and left the room. Lige's father looked from his son to the laced coffee, then blew out a ragged breath and pointed to the stove where a frypan was heating. 'Eat,' he said.

Lige took down a big breath without moving from his place near the table. 'Who are they?'

Henry Wyatt continued to stare into the coffee cup. 'Strangers, boy. Eat some supper— and don't ask so many questions.'

Lige still stood his ground. 'That one in my room's been shot in the side, up high, paw. They're outlaws, aren't they?'

Slowly, Henry Wyatt's head came up, the colour, which invariably preceded his wrath, showed, but not as dark. He nodded. 'They're outlaws.'

'Paw, that one in my room's going to die. He's burning up.'

'Well, I dug for the bullet, son, but it's too deep. He needs a doctor and there isn't one within a hundred miles of Lincoln. And even if there was...' Henry Wyatt shrugged thick shoulders. 'They let it go too long.' Then, as though speaking to himself, Lige's father said softly, 'I don't see how he did it. I don't for the life of me see how he ever got this far south.'

'From where, paw?'

'Montana.'

'Shot like that?'

'Yes,' replied Henry Wyatt, then reached for

31

the jug and laced his coffe anew. 'I don't want them here, but that one can't go another mile. Hell; he couldn't go another ten feet.'

They looked at one another in the silence that followed, then Lige went to the bucket and drank a dipperful of well-water, but he couldn't have eaten if his life had depended upon it.

The man named Harrow returned quietly, lifted the crock over his raised arm and swallowed twice, deeply, put the crock down and sank down upon the chair he'd vacated. Without looking at either of the Wyatts he rolled and lit a brown-paper cigarette. Every move he made was thorough, fluid, as deliberate and purposeful as it could be. He was very different from Lige's father who, sometimes, seemed troubled, confused, either unwilling or unable to do simple things, as though his mind couldn't relinquish some deeper hold it had.

Harrow looked up at Lige through fragrant smoke. He didn't speak, he just sat there gazing across the table.

Coyotes howled as the evening arrived, and deepened. The silence, both inside and outside, was thick enough to reach forth and feel. Eventually, Harrow arose and returned to the room of his pardner, and at about the same time Henry Wyatt arose and went off to his own bedroom, leaving the uncorked whisky jug upon the floor. Lige plugged it, and set it atop the table, then was undecided about whether to turn

32

the lamp off, or just to turn it down. He turned it down, then arranged his quilts and blankets into a suitable pallet, shucked out of his trousers, boots and shirt, and worked his way down under the blankets.

For a long while he could not sleep. But eventually he did. Once, he half-roused at some faint, muted sound in the night, but it was not repeated so he sank deeper into his purple void.

When the sky had its blue slit over against the east, Lige rolled out, dressed, took his towel and chunk of barley-lye soap and headed for the creek as he often did.

The new day had its own individual scent and feel. Since childhood Lige had thought that each day, like each person, was different. Not much, actually; different in roughly the same degree that individual people were different. They all looked pretty much the same from a distance, but up close they were different. That applied to days as well as people.

He stood a moment in the dead-hushed yard with its familiar dark-hulking log structures, and slowly turned. The birds were still drowsy in treetops over near the creek, the horses were quiet still, and those cows that had drifted in yesterday afternoon were either gone now, or were bedded down far out.

Not many creatures used the first-light time of day. Probably because the visibility was so deceptive then, a humped-up rock could turn into a hungry wolf, or a stick bent to the warmth of a log, could be a snake.

He took the pulse of this pre-day time, found nothing to bring up caution, and went on down to the creek to wash.

The water was cold, but wherever water ran shallow it wasn't unbearably cold, in summertime. Lige bathed in this same spot each Saturday morning, but only in summertime. In winter he bathed in the tub hanging unused, this time of year, upon the backwall of the cabin. He hauled water and heated it upon the stove, then jack-knifed into the tub and bathed, and it was, as he had repeatedly told his father, an awful lot of manual work for what a person got out of it. Maybe his father agreed, but all he'd ever say was, 'Suppose something happened to you, boy, and folks found you hadn't had a bath. Do like your mother said— wash all over every month in winter and every week in summer.'

He heard a sage-hen nearby, somewhere in the undergrowth, probably daintily dipping up water. If he hadn't had things on his mind he might have got a rock and stalked it. That was the best eating, roast sage-hen, and they were easy to kill.

Over a very great distance came the half-heard long cry of a wolf. If the pre-morning hadn't been so still, so fresh and receptive to sound and movement, that wolf's sounding would never have come so far. Lige guessed the critter was over against the northwesterly foothills, but the call only came once, faintly; there was no way to be sure where it had come from, exactly.

He finished washing, ducked his head to soak it, then combed back the mane of thick, coppery hair with crooked fingers and as he arose, a horse probably picked up his scent, because it nickered. He was ready for the day, and for the next half hour he did not have to do anything, if he didn't want to, but after that, when his father would rouse up and stir the fire for breakfast, Lige would start pitching out feed to the animals.

This half hour was his; no one in the world, including his father, could intrude upon it.

He went to the barn on a diagonal course, leisurely scuffing heavy dust and wondering what his father would decide about the wounded man. If they kept him, and he was an outlaw, and anyone happened along... The horse nickered again, joined this time by several others. Lige hastened a little. The moment horses heard or saw or scented man in the morning, they began demanding to be fed.

He entered the barn, which was still redolent of the nightlong darkness, and decided to feed first and kill time later. Otherwise the horses might set up such a ruckus it would awaken his father.

And Harrow.

He hadn't forgot, excactly, but they hadn't had anyone overnight in the cabin since he could remember, so he still thought only in terms of himself and his father. But the other one, the outlaw named Harrow, was over there too.

He pitched feed, and talked to the animals out back in the corrals, then went inside where the darkness clung and started choring, in there as well. In fact, because it was so dark, he forked feed into an empty stall without realizing it until, later, after everything had been fed, he ambled down to look in. The Roman-nosed big, stout sorrel horse was not there.

He returned to the outback corrals, but the sorrel gelding was not out there either. He returned to the barn, lifted blankets along the saddle-pole, found his father's rig and his own rig, then he noticed the vacant place.

Harrow was gone, then.

That opened up an entirely fresh train of thought. He and his father were going to have to tend the hurt man by themselves.

With the blue blaze widening and fresh, soft colour coming into the dawning day, Lige returned to the cabin. His father was at the stove making coffee. He looked around, then wordlessly looked away as Lige said, 'The big sorrel horse is gone.'

'Fetch some salt pork from the well-house,' mumbled his father.

Lige reached the door, then felt that

resurgence of independence he'd felt last night. He said, 'Harrow is gone, isn't he, paw?'

Henry Wyatt looked over. 'Yes. And we got a job to do, later, maybe this evening, boy. The other one's dead and we got to bury him.'

CHAPTER FIVE

FOUR HORSEMEN

They took the corpse, wrapped in soiled canvas from the barn, and put it behind the forge over in the shoeing-shed and shop, then flung old blankets and sacking over it.

Henry Wyatt said hardly a word throughout all this, and afterwards, when they returned to the house, he helped Lige put his quilts and ticking back upon the bed where the outlaw had died, and they worked, afterwards, to eliminate all sign that Harrow and the dead man had been there.

It was the first time Henry Wyatt did not seem to notice that his son was a little sharper spoken, or maybe he noticed and couldn't concentrate upon it right at the moment, but whatever it was, when Lige said, 'How did that man get shot?' his father answered without equivocation or gruffness.

'In a fight with Pinkerton detectives.'

'What did they do—that dead man and the other one?'

'Robbed an army payroll in Montana. Now don't talk about it any more. There are two hobbled horses over along the creek, northward. Saddle one of our animals and take those two several miles on the west range and turn them loose.'

Lige obeyed, as always, but when his father came out to the porch as Lige was leaving, with his worried expression, Lige felt closer to his father than he ever had before. He said, 'Don't worry; I'll take those horses where won't anyone find them.'

He could, probably, have done that without much real effort. Not many people came to the uplands this time of year. It was too early for the hunters to appear and there was no emigrant or stage road nearer than Lincoln.

He had no trouble finding the thin animals, removing their hobbles and leading them over across the creek, out through the willow-shelter to the undulating range beyond.

The heat came, gradually, as the morning wore along. The sky was cloudless and pale; looking back, he could see a faint, soft touch of green upon their ploughed ground. He also saw the fire still standing straight up from the cabin's stove-pipe.

Sixteen was young to earn manhood, but on the frontier it could come any time between fifteen and eighteen. By the time a boy was nineteen he was expected to carry a man's burden, whether he was prepared for it or not.

Lige hadn't been a man until the day before. Now he was. He would return this evening to dig a grave and bury a man. He had been spoken to almost as an equal by his father for the first time. Perhaps those weren't the true criteria, but to Lige Wyatt they were good enough, even though he did not think about it, except obliquely, except instinctively, as he rode across the empty rangeland leading the two worn-out, docile saddle animals.

Against the farthest slopes a forest stood invitingly cool but too distant. Nearer, to the north, the hills were mostly bald and low, like giant prairie-dog mounds, but grassed over and somnolent in the shimmery sunshine.

As far as Lige could see, there was nothing; no movement, no shadows, nothing but clean open country with a tilting far sweep. Motion would have caught his attention immediately, but far ahead and slightly to his right, the horsemen sat like stone, watching and holding their mounts utterly still.

Lige swung slightly southward in the general direction of a long spit of trees and came out upon the rangeland. This put everything north, and north-west, behind him. He was thinking ahead to those trees. There was a spring over there, along with shade and tall, lush grass. It was a good place for the pair of horses, who were shrunk and tucked up from hard usage. He had brought other horses to that spot. They had invariably come back fat and sassy.

But he would not cover the entire distance. The place *looked* close, but it was miles away. He got close enough, though, so that the led-animals raised their heads with interest, then he swung down, freed them, looped the lead-ropes and stepped back across leather to haze them another half mile or so at a lope, heading them in the proper direction. He did not see the riders, but he should have because now they were fanning out, were loping down-country to cut him off from home.

As he choused the loose-stock towards the spit of trees, his back was to the east, which was where the riders were completing their flanking manoeuvre. Only when he had the loose horses loping ahead directly towards the spring, did he haul around heading back.

Then he saw them.

He knew instinctively those men had deliberately slid in behind to cut him off. Fear dried his throat. He was not armed. He owned an old sixgun, but he never carried it, in fact he did not have a belt nor holster for it. His Winchester was on its pegs back at the cabin, but even if he'd had them both, the fear that closed like an iron band around his heart would have prevented him from thinking in terms of

40

fighting.

But he reacted normally; without slackening the long, loose lope of his mount, he reined southward to go out and around the farthest man. Instantly, the strangers reacted by bunching together, then breaking out in a diagonal race to cut him off.

At sixteen, when he had only been a man for one day, he thought as a rabbit not a cougar. It did not cross his mind that the horses those strangers were astride were worn down. They were too distant for him to see them that well, and now, as they started fanning out again, Lige hauled down to a halt and sat, wet-palmed and frightened.

The strangers curved westerly in a wide, flinging rush. Cold dark light shone from bared steel. Lige was frozen in time and space. His chest hurt from the fear as he waited. It did not take long. There were four of them, dusty, rumpled, weathered men as old as his father. They dropped to a walk a half mile out. At a quarter mile, guns bristling, one of them said harshly, 'It's a damned kid.'

They came up and halted. The heavy-set, pale-eyed one out front spat amber, holstered his Colt, clasped both hands atop the horn and said, 'Boy, where did you get those two horses you run towards the trees?'

Lige's voice failed him exactly as it had when he'd ridden up unexpectedly on Harrow the day before. He couldn't make his thoughts come down into words.

The heavy-set man was cruel-eyed with a wound for a mouth. The other three, wearing suit-coats instead of rangemen's rough shirts, sat studying Lige. One of them, a lean-faced mahogany-coloured man with a drooping dragoon moustache, said, 'What's your name, boy?'

The answer to that came naturally, but still, not without a little hesitancy. 'Lige Wyatt, sir.'

'You live yonder at that ranch with the log building, do you, Lige?'

'Yes sir.'

The heavy-set man turned aside and spat dark again, shifted his cud of chewing tobacco and loosened in the saddle, content to leave this to the man with the dragoon moustache. The others loosened, too. They had no reason not to; a sixteen-year-old wasn't too much of a threat when he was armed, and this one had nothing more dangerous than a pair of lead-ropes looped around his saddlehorn.

The man with the drooping moustache said, 'Where did you find those two horses, Lige?'

The answer to that, obviously, would drive Lige into a corner. He would have lied if he could have thought of a plausible prevarication. He sat, waiting for something to come to mind, and meanwhile the heavy-set man removed his hat, mopped a fish-belly forehead, re-settled the dusty hat and said, 'Come along. Let's go back to the claim. That's what it is, isn't it, boy, a squatter's land claim where you'n your folks live?'

Lige answered that the way he had heard other people answer it. 'A homestead. My folks came out from Missouri and staked it.'

One of the other men, dark-eyed and hard-looking, said, 'Lige, you got any older brothers down there to the house?'

'No sir.'

'Anyone down there besides your folks, then?'

'No sir. Just my paw. My mother died three years back. She's—buried near the creek.'

The heavy-set man, reinhand raised, did not signal the horse for a moment longer. He sat, studying Lige Wyatt, then he finally reined around, speaking to the others as he did so.

'Hell; we'll have to make arrangements for the boy.'

Whatever that meant, the others seemed to silently agree as they all started walking their horses in the direction of the cabin. It was the man with the droopy moustache who rode stirrup with Lige. For a while he was quiet, like the others, sitting erect studying the landfall to the east where the log buildings were, and beyond. But eventually he said, sounding tired, 'Where are the two fellers who rode those horses, Lige, if they aren't up yonder in the

43

cabin?'

The sourness left Lige's throat as suddenly as it had come, and the iron band loosened inside his chest. He looked around. 'Who are you—sir?'

The stranger fished inside a pocket and brought forth a nickel-steel circlet with a star inside it. 'The law,' he said simply, and dropped the badge back out of sight. 'Lige, if those two fellers are up yonder inside the cabin with your pappy, someone's likely to get hurt. Maybe your paw.'

There could be no harm in avoiding this possibility. 'No sir, they aren't at the house.'

The heavy-set man twisted in his saddle. 'You telling the truth, boy?' he growled.

Lige answered without fear. 'Yes sir.' He groped for an evasive word, and found it by simply omitting the *whole* truth, by simply dropping the first word. 'Rode out some time last night. I don't know when, except that when I went to do the chores this morning there was no sign.'

The four men fell silent as their horses plodded along. Lige found courage, somewhere, and considered jumping out his horse, which was fresh and strong. The horses around him were ridden down. But the holstered guns around him decided him against breaking for it; a man might out-run another man's horse, but not his bullets.

44

Maybe, if his father was watching by now, he'd see them coming, and escape. They could never catch him from this far out, if he took a strong horse.

But no one showed up ahead in the yard where bright, dazzling hot brilliance limned everything perfectly. When they were still a fair distance out the heavy-set man raised a thick arm. 'Cort,' he said to the man with the dragoon moustache, 'take the south side.' To the remaining pair of lawmen he said, 'Cover the north and east. I'll go directly in with the boy. We'll come through the back of the barn.'

Cort studied the cabin and barn, acting as though he had not heard the orders. 'Ben, you're taking a bad chance. Even if there's only one, he's forted up in there by now.'

The heavy-set man, Ben Farley, a U.S. Marshal, simply shrugged mighty shoulders. 'I've had to do a damned sight worse, and without a kid along to keep someone from shooting. There's no other way. Look at that place. The barn's too far from the house. You can't approach that cabin except across open ground.' Ben Farley cast a sardonic glance at Lige. 'Your pappy must have had reason for building like he did, eh, boy?'

Lige gave the only answer to that he'd ever heard. 'The well was over there by the cabin, sir. It was a spring and we dug it out. That's why we built the cabin where it is.'

45

They were close enough for the other men to start angling away. Cort looked over and said, 'Lige, be sensible.' That's all he said, then he lifted his tired mount into a lope and left the others. When only Lige and the heavy-set man were riding directly onward, the lawman let his horse drop its head, reins swinging, and concentrated hard upon the cabin. 'Tell me about your paw,' he said, not unkindly. 'Did he know those two who rode in on them horses you left yonder?'

Lige could answer that truthfully, too. 'No sir. In fact it was me that found them. I was out hunting yonder towards the bald hills northeasterly, and I rode right up on to this man in a sort of fog and didn't even see him until—'

'Was one of them hurt, Lige?'

'Yes sir.' Lige locked his mouth closed.

The burly man did not notice, he was concentrating, now, upon the dark interior of the barn, which lay only a pistol-shot ahead.

CHAPTER SIX

THE SECRET IS REVEALED

His father was not there!

Ben Farley stayed in the barn for a while, trying to make up his mind about crossing that

46

open ground. Finally, he said, 'Lige, you go on up to the house. And you tell your paw there is a U.S. Marshal here in the barn, with three deputy U.S. Marshals. You tell him we've got the place covered from four sides. I want to talk to him. That's all. If he's got nothing to hide, why then you can tell him he's got nothing to worry about. Do you understand?'

Lige nodded, then teetered in the half-light, half-shadow of the barn's front opening looking towards the cabin. He knew his father would not shoot as long as Lige was exposed, but by now he was certain his father had the old .45–.70 lying over a sill, waiting.

Marshal Farley said, 'Go on, boy. No one's going to pot-shoot you. And remember exactly what I said for you to tell your paw.'

Lige struck out. The heat made sweat run under his shirt. Once, he twisted and looked beyond the yard, as he walked. The motionless horsemen were out there. Now, there was no way for his father to escape. He squeezed both fists so tightly that the nails gouged the flesh. The earlier fear was entirely gone, now that he had the log walls dead ahead and his father in there. The two of them could fight off four men from inside.

At the door he got his first inkling; it was slightly ajar. He pushed it open, stepped inside, saw the .45–.70 upon its pegs, felt the emptiness of the cabin, and with a sinking heart, went

47

from room to room. His father was not in the house.

Perhaps he should have been elated, but now he was alone again. He did not want to fight those men alone. He dipped up water at the kitchen bucket, drank deeply, felt fresh perspiration start out all over his body, and dropped weak-legged down upon the chair Harrow had used only the evening before.

Perhaps his father had seen them capture Lige, and had fled. For some reason he did not believe this had happened. He could sense a more lingering, a deeper, kind of emptiness to the cabin, which meant his father had been gone longer than just the last hour or so.

He guessed his father must have ridden out only a short while after Lige had left to take those horses out several miles westward.

From the barn a man's raw call brought into fresh focus Lige's predicament. He arose, went to the door and leaned there, one arm upon the trim. 'No one is here,' he sang out, expecting Marshal Farley to emerge from the barn. Echoes bounced back and forth from his call. No one appeared in the yard.

He walked out under the warped wooden overhang which was their porch. 'Mister,' he called towards the barn. 'He's gone. He's not in here.'

This time there was a reply. 'Lige; step ahead a few yards, then stand still, facing the barn.

48

Come ahead now.'

Lige obeyed. Marshal Farley stepped out of the barn keeping Lige between himself and the cabin, walking cat-footed, balanced forward, with a cocked Colt in his thick right fist. He came all the way, then peered past with a puzzled expression. 'No one's in there, boy?'

'I already told you, twice. He's not in there.'

Lige preceded the lawman to the door. Ben Farley peered in first, then stepped in. He reached to shove Lige aside and stalked from the room, the cocked Colt steady and poised to kill. When he returned to the parlour he lowered the gun and scowled. For a moment he stood in deep thought, then he marched back outside and wig-wagged with his arms, the Colt upraised and still clenched.

The sun burned down through long silence until those mounted lawmen loped in close to the cabin. Lige watched from the doorway. Ben Farley stated conditions in a flat tone of voice. 'Maybe he saw us coming. Maybe he just rode out. Anyway, the day's nearly spent so we might as well settle in right here. Maybe he'll come back.'

One of the deputy marshals said, 'Lincoln's downcountry a piece, Marshal. I can get down there before dark, and if he's there, I can arrest him and have the constable jail him.'

'How?' demanded Marshal Farley. 'You don't know what he looks like. You go to asking

49

around, and someone down there'll find Wyatt first and—'

'I've been at this eleven years,' said the deputy, testily.

Ben Farley yielded. 'Go ahead. But Matt, be damned careful. And get back as soon as you've got something definite.'

This lawman re-mounted and headed around the house in the direction of town. Farley turned to the other man whose name Lige did not know, and said, 'Stay circling out a piece, Alfred. Anyone at all comes riding towards this place—nail him.'

Finally, Marshal Farley said, 'Cort, look the buildings over. What the hell, we got nothing else to do and it's getting along. When you've finished come on up the house. We'll rassle up something to eat.'

Farley came up where Lige was standing, and scowled. He looked cruel, but perhaps that couldn't be helped, maybe his face had just set up that way after lifelong hardship and danger. For a fact, except when Lige hadn't answered him, or had been slow in answering, Marshal Ben Farley had not been too harsh, and once, at least, when Lige had mentioned his mother, the lawman had looked almost understanding.

He pointed to the chair out front. 'Sit, boy,' and when Lige hesitated he said, 'Well; you been raised right anyway,' and took the chair himself, shoved back his hat, let his body turn loose in the shaded comfort, and gave another order. 'Step around in front of me, Lige. That's fine. Now tell me—if your pappy went off to pay a call, where would he be most apt to go?'

There was no place, unless it would be down to town, but usually, when his father had made that trip, he'd taken Lige along. 'I don't know, sir. Our nearest neighbour is—'

'Yeah, I know,' broke in the lawman. 'We scouted up the countryside. You folks are isolated, up here. But maybe he saw us coming. Where would he go if he did that?'

Lige had no clear idea. 'Well; anywhere, I reckon—sir. Except that he don't very often go off without me, or at least telling me when he's liable to be back.'

Marshal Farley kept a steady, hard gaze upon Lige. 'Do you know what I saw in that barn, boy, and what I saw out back of it?'

'No sir.'

Farley loosened his coat, swung the chair back as Henry Wyatt usually did of an evening on the porch, and got thoroughly comfortable before he spoke again.

'Horses, boy, with brands on 'em from Idaho, from Montana, from a lot of different places. You know what else?'

'No sir,' replied Lige, his voice beginning to fade.

'A saddle, boy.' Marshal Farley kept staring, boring his eyes into Lige. 'There's a saddle on

51

the pole down there, Lige—with dried blood on it. Lots of dried blood. The carbine's still in the boot. There was a blanket-roll behind the cantle.'

Lige felt for the upright at his back and leaned for sudden support upon it.

Cort came strolling up to the cabin, thumbs hooked in his shellbelt. He looked as impassive as a stone but his eyes were dead-level upon Lige, even though he addressed the U.S. Marshal.

'Ben . . . Frank Harrow is over yonder in the shop behind a forge, covered with old rags and wrapped in a wagon-canvas.'

The words fell like steel against glass. Lige could not take his eyes off the burly chieftain of these lawmen. He was weak, but he was as fascinated as a bird before a snake. Marshal Farley turned his head slightly towards Lige. For a moment he was silent, then he crashed down off the wall and lunged up to his feet. 'Come along,' he told Lige, and reached to give him a slight push.

Not a word was said, and in the quiet of the empty world their bootfalls made grinding sounds through dust and mica.

Cort had dragged the body out, had uncovered it. Lige looked, then looked away, his stomach balling up with queasiness. Marshal Farley leaned, poked at the wound, and pulled back saying, 'Cort, how in the hell did he ever

52

manage to hang on this long? I tell you, those wanted flyers only told half the story. They're the toughest pair I ever shagged after.'

Evidently Cort was not thinking along those lines. He turned, thumbs hooked again, and said, 'Lige; how many cows does your paw run?'

It was such an unexpected and guileless question. 'Thirty head, sir.'

'And he farms that patch yonder—maybe thirty acres?'

'Yes sir; to wheat and oats and barley for feed.'

Cort faced Marshal Farley. 'These folks don't make it off any thirty head of cows, Ben, even if they actually brand that many. And they sure as hell can't make it off thirty acres of grain hay. Ben; this feller Wyatt's sellin' and tradin' horses to outlaws. Did you study the brands on the animals in the corrals?'

'I saw them, yes.'

'You've got the flyers in your saddlebags. They list the brands on the horses some of those outlaws were riding. I'll make you a bet.'

Marshall Farley did not answer Cort's proposal, he instead reached and half spun Lige towards him. 'Boy, is that what your pappy does?'

Lige was angered. Not by the implication, but by the childish tears that burned his eyes. He was cornered. Maybe he was even going to be shot by these lawmen. But his father would get dark in the face if he could see Lige now, fighting to keep his lips from trembling, with his swimming vision, with his stomach churning all over again.

'We work our cattle,' he flung defiantly at the heavy-set man, 'and we work our ground, and we get by, and take your hand off'n my shoulder.' As he said the last, Lige whipped away, twisting from the closing fingers. Marshal Farley hadn't been fast enough, probably because he hadn't expected anything like this. He'd had no reason to expect it, up until now Lige had been docile, obviously badly frightened, but not like he was now.

Cort was quicker. Lige would have whirled to race for the cabin where the guns were, but Deputy Cort Lane collared him before he could get untracked and turned. He hauled him back with seemingly very little effort, even though Deputy Lane did not look especially strong. He settled him, hard, against the wall near the dead man.

'Settle down,' he said severely, the way a man speaks to a fighting colt. 'Lige, get hold of yourself.'

But it was too late. The fear, the dread, all the strain broke out. Lige swore at them, something he had never been allowed to do around his father, not even when he got horse-tromped or horse-kicked. When they stood, immovably blocking his escape, and hardly changed

54

expression, Lige's outcries beat away upon the still, hot air without doing any harm at all.

He ran out of breath, finally, and they let him move clear of the sightless, dry eyes below. He felt as though he had run an uphill mile, his chest burned for air.

Marshal Farley stooped for a final glance at the wound in the dead man's side, then shaking his head, he flipped the filthy old canvas back into place, shutting out the dead man's grey, rigid, sunken face.

'Boy,' he said to Lige, 'we're going up to the house and get something to eat, then we're going to set and wait. If your pappy comes in, fine, if he don't, well, maybe they'll pick him up in Lincoln, or maybe he'll ride into someone on his way in. And boy, one more thing; you're big as any of us. That means you're big enough to hang. Big enough to shoot if you try and run, or reach for a weapon. Now then, walk ahead of us to the house. What've you got on hand for supper?'

Lige was made sick by the talk of food while they were standing over that stone-cold dead man. He was also demoralized and defeated. Without letting on that he had heard a word of what the lawman had said, he started back in the direction of the cabin, with his entire world in ruins.

CHAPTER SEVEN

THE LONG NIGHT BEGINS

There was a dead-time after the discovery of the body in the shoeing shed. The pair of older men, tough as they obviously were, may have been in the saddle for a long time, although Lige had no way of knowing that except by their appearance, but in any case, when they went to work making themselves and Lige a meal, they hardly talked and their movements were sluggish.

When Lige said it was time for him to go down to the barn and feed, Marshal Farley growled.

'That'll keep. You just stay where you are.'

Again, a little later when Deputy Marshal Cort Lane happened to catch Lige eyeing his father's .45-.70 on its wall-pegs, he did not say a word, he simply looked Lige squarely in the eyes, and shook his head with deceptively mild finality.

What the pair of lawmen prepared was in fact not any worse than most of Henry Wyatt's meals, but it half-disgusted Lige to stand there watching them eat as though they hadn't just been gazing upon a wasted corpse. When they told him to fill up a plate, he declined and continued to stand silently, while the full force of night eventually arrived.

It was the silence perhaps even more than the uncertainty that kept Lige existing between hope and despair, alternating weakly between one and the other. As time passed, he came to the solemn conclusion that his father had either gone down to Lincoln, or had struck out for the northward mountains. If the latter, then he was sure his father had seen four strangers and had guessed who they were.

But if his father had simply decided to make a quick trip to town—and hadn't come back by now—with each fresh-settling layer of nightfall the possibility increased that Marshal Farley's deputy down in Lincoln had made his apprehension. At the worst, perhaps the deputy had shot his father by now.

Lige sank down upon a bench near the stove, some distance from the closed door leading outside. For one day he had been a man, and the kind of burden that now bowed his spirit confirmed the aging, even though it had nothing to do with his years.

Cort Lane arose and stepped to the doorway, moved outside so as not to be light-limned, remained outside briefly, then returned. 'Thought I heard riders,' he told Marshal Farley. 'They're heading for the barn and are coming in from the east. I'll go take a stand down there. One of us has to keep an eye on the boy.'

Marshal Farley nodded and reached for more coffee. He seemed willing to listen to this particular deputy, and to assent when he made a suggestion. Lige had noticed that earlier, in broad daylight. Sometimes it was almost as though Cort Lane were the U.S. Marshal, and Ben Farley were the Deputy U.S. Marshal.

After Cort left, Farley skidded his chair around and thoughtfully studied Lige. 'I'll tell you something I learned many years ago, boy. No matter what you've been through, when a chance to eat comes up, take it. No matter what else is going on, eat-up when you have the opportunity, because sometimes it can get downright painfully long between meals.'

Lige looked away. Perhaps Marshal Farley's philosophy was sound, but it inspired deep disgust in Lige.

Farley understood. As he whittled off a corner of cut-plug with a wicked-bladed pocket-knife, then put up both knife and plug, and pouched the tobacco into one cheek, he said, 'You folks came from Missouri?'

Lige nodded.

'Back there, what did your pappy do for a living?'

Lige said, 'Farmed, mostly, and made buggies in a shed near where we lived.'

Ben Farley's steady, hard eyes showed interest. 'You don't say. Made buggies? Why

58

didn't he do that out here; seems to me there's a call for wagonmakers and such like.'

'He didn't like the towns,' replied Lige, repeating the reason he had heard his father give quite often. 'He wanted to come west.'

Farley masticated his cud and gently inclined his head indicating, perhaps, that he did not like towns either. 'And when you folks got out here,' he surmised from much experience and much observation, 'it was all different, and hard, wasn't it?'

Lige could agree with that without a single qualm. It *had* been hard, very hard, in fact, for not only the first year, but for most of the second year. He regarded Marshal Farley with a blend of dislike, suspicion, fear and now, a feeling that they did, after all, have something in common although he could not have said what it was.

'It was hard, yes sir, but we came through like my mother said we would. We kept warm and we ate ... Sometimes, we didn't eat real good.' He began to lose his dread of Farley a little. 'They didn't like us down in Lincoln. None of us; they just don't like homesteaders down there.'

Farley continued to eye the youth, and to also masticate. 'You got to understand, son, that this has always been the cowman's country.'

'He don't own it,' exclaimed Lige, repeating, parrot-like, what all homesteaders invariably

59

replied to this kind of logic. 'We got as much right as he has.'

Marshal Farley re-filled his coffee cup, swilled a little and put the cup aside. During this interlude he had apparently decided not to pursue this topic, because when he spoke again, he said, 'Your folks ever hear that their claim was on one of the north-south outlaw trails?'

'No sir,' answered Lige, not yielding so much as a blink in their little staring match. Now, he knew why Marshal Farley was being amiable; he had been leading up to this particular point; he was relying upon his having won Lige's confidence, or friendship, or something, so that when he guided the conversation to where he could encourage Lige to incriminate Henry Wyatt, it would happen as naturally as falling off a log.

'You folks saw a rider sneak past now and again,' stated Marshal Farley. 'You couldn't hardly help seeing that.' Farley settled back and sipped more coffee before continuing. 'You know, Lige, my boys and I've been fifteen days on the trail of that dead man out in your shed, and his brother, and along the way we've learnt a lot of things. This place of your pappy's is smack-dab made to order for what your pappy's been doing. We run across other places, only a couple of them because it's a chancy business, what your pappy's been doing, but we run across some others doing the same thing.'

Lige burned to ask what had happened at those other places, but he also realized that the moment he showed that kind of interest, Marshal Farley, already as suspicious as a man could get, would have his suspicions either fully confirmed, or at least immensely reinforced. He sat and said nothing.

Someone whistled from the yard. Ben Farley, for all his thickness and the relaxed, loose way he had been sitting for the past half hour, was on his feet and moving doorward, gun in hand, with astonishing speed and grace. Lige was too surprised to do more than stare.

The whistle came again, a soft sort of trilling sound. Farley opened the door a crack and remained behind it. 'Cort. . . ?'

'Yeah. Matt's got something you'd like to see.'

'Come in,' called Farley, and took two backward steps, raised his Colt and cocked it.

Lige held his breath, but when Cort pushed inside and saw the gun aimed at his middle, he practically ignored it and turned to watch someone else enter.

The last man in was one of those other deputies, the man Lige had heard the Marshal call Matt; he was the deputy who had been set to watching from out in the night. In front of the deputy marshal was a thin, youngish, dust-stained man who could have been in his middle twenties. He had a holster tied down, but there

61

was no gun in it.

Lige knew without being told who that disarmed stranger was—another duskrider. This time, though, instead of meeting Henry Wyatt, the fugitive outlaw had ridden into Marshal Farley's trap and had been caught and disarmed.

Farley put up his weapon and studied the captive. 'Well, well; you were just riding in to pay a neighbourly call,' he said, not unkindly, although his eyes were coldly staring and his slit of a mouth was sucked flat. 'What's your name?'

The thin man said, 'Joe Smith,' and Cort knocked him down; he hit the edge of the door with his back, half turned into the log wall, and fell, tangled in his own tracks. It happened so fast Lige did not see the blow at all.

Farley asked again. 'What is your name?'

The man on the floor stared from pale eyes, and shook the cobwebs out of his mind as he slowly regained his feet. He put a soiled hand to his jaw. 'Jim Swain,' he muttered.

Marshal Farley nodded. 'Yeah. I've seen the flyers on you.' He looked at Matt. 'How'd you get him?'

'No trouble at all,' the deputy replied. 'I heard his horse and went up on foot, let him come to me, then threw down on him.' Matt looked at the fugitive. 'Tell him how you happened along, down here.'

The outlaw flicked a glance at Lige, at the jug

on the table, at the coffeepot, and said, 'I give a feller up in Miles City ten dollars and he give me a map on how to find this here homestead.'

The deputy named Matt fished out a stained, limp piece of paper and passed it across to Marshal Farley. 'He had it in his pocket when I shook him down. Look at the name writ down below the X where the homestead is.'

Farley looked, and read the name aloud. 'Henry Wyatt.'

Lige saw his last small hope whisk out. If there had ever been much chance for his father to talk his way clear, it had just vanished.

Farley carefully folded the map and just as carefully tucked it into his left-hand shirt-pocket. 'Have some coffee,' he said to the outlaw, gesturing towards the table. 'Lige; fill a cup for Jim Swain, who, if I recollect it right, is wanted in Nebraska and Montana for murder.'

Lige looked at the outlaw, and was in turn ignored as Jim Swain went to the table and sank tiredly down, still gingerly feeling his jaw where he had been struck. As Lige filled a tin cup and pushed it over, the outlaw, still without looking, picked up the cup and drank.

He reminded Lige of a badger he had once caught and caged; Swain did not react to capture with shouts of defiance, he simply sat there, relaxed and looking around, studying the cabin, the men who had him in custody, and finally he fished forth the makings and rolled a smoke. He was a professional outlaw with the calm and secret thought-processes of all professional men, inside the law or outside it. Finally, evidently feeling better, he said, 'Who are you?' to Marshal Farley. After he had his answer he blew smoke and let his gaze wander impassively to the man who had knocked him down. He did not say anything at all; the look said it all for him.

Farley sent Cort and Matt over to the shoeing shed where there were chains, with orders to lock their captive in. He then said for Matt to resume his vigil out on the range from the buildings, just in case someone else might ride up like Jim Swain had done.

His last orders to Cort were: 'Al ought to be riding in before too long, hadn't he? How far is that damned town from here anyway?'

Cort answered with indifference, 'Few miles. I'll go out a ways and see if I can pick up any sound coming from the south.'

After the three men left, Marshal Farley continued to chew his cud and to drink coffee. But now he was thoughtful, and seemed unaware that Lige was even in the kitchen with him.

Finally, though, as he was standing, cup in his left hand, looking up at the old .45-.70 on the wall-pegs, he said, 'Lige, you don't ever have to like a man to heed what he says. Listen to me,' the hard, cruel eyes came down. 'You've seen enough today to figure it out; there isn't much of a chance for a man to make outlawry pay. Some manage it, but damned precious few. I know—you hate my guts for what I'm going to do when we get our hands on your pappy. Well; that's only right and proper, because he's your father and all. But you remember this, boy: You got to learn from the mistakes of men like your father—and Jim Swain, and the Harrow brothers—because no man lives long enough to make all the mistakes himself. You remember that. You aren't going to live long enough to learn from all the mistakes you yourself can make, so learn from the mistakes of others.'

CHAPTER EIGHT

DIFFERENT KINDS OF MEN

It was good advice, but Marshal Farley probably did not hold out much hope that Lige would heed it, at least not under the present circumstances when he was too concerned over the plight of his father. But if he lived long enough, and got wise enough, he might work it into his personal philosophy.

At the moment Marshal Farley gave his advice Lige was slouching in tired silence wondering when the lawmen would leave, wondering what they had in mind for him; whether they found his father or not, what they intended to do before dawn. He had it in mind, for no particular reason, that they would not remain at the claim any longer than dawn.

Cort returned, eventually, with a chill beginning to come into the night, and sank heavily down at the table. 'No sign of Al,' he reported to Ben Farley.

For a moment those two gazed at one another, then Farley got up, fetched the coffeepot from the stove, filled the two cups, then sat down again. 'Maybe he got attracted by the town. It's been a long while, Cort . . .'

For a while the man with the droopy dragoon moustache simply sipped coffee, but eventually he said, 'I'm going to bed down out in the barn. When Matt comes in—and if Al gets back before daylight—they'd better do the same, Ben. No telling where this damned trail will take us tomorrow, and we can't ride it falling asleep in the saddle.' He arose and finished his coffee, then his glance fell upon Lige. For a moment Cort stood in silence, then he spoke to Lige. 'Boy, it don't look to me like your paw's coming back. You'd better think on that, and by morning figure out what you've got to do—on your own.'

Cort left the cabin. For a while afterwards Farley sat staring at his boot toes, but eventually he arose with a sigh and said, 'Come along, boy.

66

We all got to get some rest, but you're the youngest and therefore the one that'll need the least of it, so I'll chain you in, too, just in case you had some notion about riding out.'

They left the cabin. The night was fast losing its residue of daylong heat, which meant it had to be getting along; Lige did not know, exactly, what time it was, but he guessed it to be about ten o'clock.

At the shoeing-shed the outlaw, Swain, sat chained in a corner with a salt-stiff saddleblanket around his shoulders. The corpse of Harrow the outlaw had been rolled over into a dark corner, but to Lige, it loomed sinisterly large and lumpy even in the darkness.

Swain and Farley exchanged a look, and did not speak as Farley gathered some lengths of wagon-chain and secured them around Lige's ankles, then moved behind and did the same with his wrists.

Lige sat with his back to the rough planks of the shed's north wall. He had a fair view of the yard across to the west, where the barn was, and southward where the cabin was. There were plenty of stars to add their light to the moonglow, so visibility was not too bad. But there was nothing to see that Lige hadn't been looking at ever since he could remember.

Farley left, heading across for the barn, evidently to palaver with Cort. He hadn't quite reached the barn when the outlaw seated nearby, addressed Lige in a hard, quiet voice.

'What're they going to do?'

'Rest until about dawn, then leave, I guess,' Lige replied. 'But there's still that one down in town. The one they call Al.' Lige turned towards Swain. 'He's looking for my father down there.'

Swain pulled the old blanket closer round his shoulders. 'You'd better hope they don't find him,' he grumbled. 'Where in hell did they come from? I didn't have no warning at all; one minute I was slippin' in, down here, and the next minute that feller rose up out of the grass.'

Lige related how he had met the four men. He could talk easily to the outlaw, and Swain rolled a cigarette with his chained hands, lit it, and blew a big smokey sigh as he said, 'If your paw's got a lick of sense he won't even look back until he's crossing the line over into Mexico.'

Lige gazed steadily at Swain. The man's face was narrow, dark, and hard. He meant exactly what he had just said. In Henry Wyatt's position that is exactly what he would have done. It made Lige's heart sink a little, even though he struggled to convince himself his father wouldn't do that, wouldn't abandon him like that.

A horseman entered the yard, over by the barn, dismounted stiffly and led his animal inside. It was hard to tell in the night, but Lige thought that had to be the man called Matt.

Swain watched, too, then he said, 'Be nice to give them fellers an hour to get sound asleep, then burn that gawdamned barn down around their ears.'

Lige leaned back, closed his eyes, and tried to clear his mind for sleep, but he could not do it. There was still that other one, the man called Alfred, somewhere, either down in Lincoln or on the range somewhere, searching for his father.

In all the years of his life, including the bad first couple of years out here on the homestead in Wyoming, Lige had never felt as he did now. Alone. Cut off from everything he had always been able to hold to. It was a terrifying experience. If he had been able to concentrate on that alone, he might have wept despite himself, and yet actually he was about as self-sufficient as he would ever be. He knew every trick for living off the land. On his day-long hunts he became as adept as an Indian at making his own way. But that wasn't it; he wouldn't have cried for himself as much as he'd have cried for what had been taken from him. First his mother, now his father, and probably by morning, the homestead as well.

It was improbable that if his father had abandoned him, he'd ever be able to keep the claim. Regardless of his rights to it, he was not, in the eyes of others, that much of a man yet, and while the claim wasn't really worth much in the eyes of others, homesteaders as well as local cowmen, it was still worth *something*, particularly to the cattlemen who were always seeking to augment their hold on more and more rangeland.

'Rider coming,' grumbled Swain from his corner.

Lige came out of his reverie with a beating heart. He *hadn't* been abandoned, then. But when he tried to detect the sound, he failed. For a full couple of minutes he heard nothing. Eventually he picked up the sound, though, and as he listened, he also wondered at the outlaw's ability to hear so well. It was almost uncanny.

Swain said, 'It won't be your paw, boy, not this time. This feller's riding in just like he knows what's going on.'

That, also, was a good observation. Evidently Jim Swain's way of thinking was pitched to the night; to the ways of survival for a man of his kind, and experience had sharpened all his senses.

The oncoming horseman did not make much sound, but in the kind of late-night utter silence which filled the area, even that soft-cadenced walk of his shod horse was loud enough. Then the sound ceased quite abruptly.

Swain guessed again. 'He come to the barn from out back. Now then, if he's the one from town, that'll be all there is to it. If he isn't— you're going to hear someone get shot directly.'

70

There were no gunshots. There was no additional sound at all for a half hour and longer. Lige strained forward to hear. His older companion in the dark corner settled back to get as comfortable as possible, and said, 'Forget it, boy. That's got to be the fourth one. Now they're all together snug as ticks on a fat cow over there in the barn. And here we are, chained tight, or we could steal horses, fire the barn, and get out of this lousy country.'

Lige gave it up, eventually. Swain was right again, apparently. It was too dark inside the shed to see the chained outlaw very well, except as a pale blur where his face was, and a hunched up lump where his body was. Lige began to transfer some of his reliance to Swain. He said, 'There should be a way to get loose.'

The outlaw grunted a cold laugh. 'This is chain we're done up in, boy, not rope. There's a padlock on my ankles with the loops made fast to my wrists as well. Did you ever hear of anyone gnawing through wagon-chain?' As though that topic did not warrant any more, the outlaw said, 'If your paw'd been around, I'd have been able to make it all the way down to New Mexico. One more horse would have done it.' Swain settled back a little, making rattling sounds as his body moved. 'I'd have been home safe in another week of steady riding.' He sat in his reveries for a moment without speaking, then he said, 'Six thousand dollars and home

71

free. It's a lousy fate that turns a man like this.' He raised his arms to make the chain rattle. 'It isn't men that'll get the best of you, boy, it's fate, life, some gawdamned vicious destiny that commences when you're just a kid, making it harder for you. People only lend fate a hand; they try to keep you down, where fate shoves you. This was my last trip. I had enough money. And here I am, not even half way. Do you know what happens to me now, boy?'

Lige knew because he had heard what Marshal Farley had accused Swain of: Murder. But he did not answer, so the outlaw spoke again as though he hadn't wanted, or needed an answer.

'Hangrope, that's what, boy. They'll hang me in some lousy cowtown. What'd you say the name of the nearest town was?'

'Lincoln.'

'Well; accordin' to the law you got to try a man and convict him where he committed his crimes. That would be back in Montana or over in Nebraska. But I'll make you a bet, they'll hang me down there in Lincoln.'

'How can they do that?' asked Lige, and Jim Swain gave that death-rattle laugh again.

'Easy, boy. Real easy. They just fit the rope round your gullet and drag you up. They got plenty of time afterwards to figure out what capital crime I committed in Wyoming.'

That sounded too cynical even for Lige, but

72

he was inclined to believe, simply because Swain had proven himself a man capable of discerning things like invisible riders in the night.

Lige had been getting an awful lot of education this day and this night. More, probably, than he would ever get again in his entire lifetime. Being a man laid a considerable burden upon a person.

Swain said, 'How come your paw to get into this business of peddling horses to fellers riding through?'

Lige's answer was based on what he had figured out, this past year or so, plus what he had heard Farley and the other men say over at the cabin. He did not *like* saying it, because it put into words what he did not want to believe about his father, actually, but he *did* put it into words.

'Fellers come riding through now and then. I guess my father sold a few horses for a good price without maybe really thinking about it too much, at first. Lately, it seemed like duskriders just naturally came along. Did someone up in Montana really give you that map, and tell you my paw'd sell you a fresh horse?'

Swain looked over. 'Of course they did. That's a silly damned question. How else would I have known to come here, boy?' Swain waited, and when Lige did not speak again, Swain said, 'You figure your paw's a bad man, don't you? Well, bad means you got caught, and good

73

means you done the same things only you *didn't* get caught.'

Lige knew that was not true. He sat and thought about Jim Swain, and came to a sound judgement of the outlaw; maybe Swain had always been cold and hard, and maybe, as he'd hinted earlier, he had developed into this kind of a man only gradually. But one thing seemed certain, he was now unalterably dedicated to outlawry, and he now had a good-sounding justification for everything he did. All of it was wrong, but it *sounded* right, the way Swain told it.

Swain believed his own lies, Lige thought, and marvelled at that. His education was progressing; tonight he had learned about five different kinds of men. If he included his father, the number would be six men, but he didn't lump his father with the others. Not yet, anyway. He might have to do that by dawn, but it wasn't even midnight yet.

He closed his eyes, and finally, when it was too late to do anything about it, he felt hungry.

CHAPTER NINE

END OF THE LONG NIGHT

Cort and the man called Matt were in the shoeing shed when Lige awakened, taking the chains off Swain. It was the inevitable rattling that awakened him. He did not move, except his eyes, and for a nightmarish moment he could not sort out his jumbled thoughts and remember who these men all were.

Then it came back in a rush.

Cort growled for Swain to stand. The outlaw obeyed in stony silence, but his joints were stiff so he had to lean upon the anvil for a few moments, and meanwhile Cort turned to free Lige. When that was done and the youth also stood up, as tall as any of them, but only half as thick, Cort said, 'We're going to eat, then we're heading out. Walk over to the cabin and don't get cute. Either one of you.'

There was a light at the cabin, just one and it came from the kitchen. As Lige trudged beside Swain he wondered, briefly, why Farley hadn't supervised their release instead of Cort; why, Farley, who was the chieftain, would be over there doing the cooking.

He was wrong. As soon as they all trooped inside he saw how wrong he had been. It wasn't

75

Farley at the cookstove, it was the man they called Al, the one who had ridden down to Lincoln looking for Henry Wyatt. Farley was having a smoke and a pre-breakfast cup of black coffee. Lige had always thought that his father was a heavy coffee drinker, but any one of these men seemed to drink twice as much.

Marshal Farley was brisk this morning. While Swain and Lige were still sleep-numbed, he said, 'We'll be heading out in an hour, when we're through eating. We're going south to Lincoln. Swain, you stay there in charge of the town marshal. We'll send a letter back to Montana about you, and I reckon they'll want you extradited. Boy; you're going to stay down there with the marshal too. He don't know it yet, but that's it.' Farley gazed a little longer at Lige, then said, 'Your paw passed through Lincoln last night, early. He didn't stay. A few folks saw him heading southward.' Again Farley paused. 'Well, son, I don't know what else to do about you. Can't set you loose, in case you know where your paw is, or in case you try something foolish, maybe a bushwhack or something.' Farley flapped his arms indicating this topic was not only distasteful to him, but that it also was something he wanted to be finished with. To Lige, the discussion so far lightened his anxieties a lot; his father was still free, Al had not caught him in town, he had not arrested nor shot him.

It would be humiliating to be locked up in Lincoln jailhouse. Folks would hear about all this, now, and both he and his father would be dishonoured, which was bitter to contemplate, but maybe, when Farley and his deputies were gone, they wouldn't hold him in the jailhouse very long, then he could streak it on southward in search of his father.

'Eat,' commanded Al, who had been doing the cooking, with a flour-sack tucked into his gunbelt, and with his hat on, a fat cigarette in his mouth, and his spurs on as though he were doing this only very temporarily, and would fling down the flour-sack in the very next instant and dash for his horse.

It was a little crowded at the table, which his father had only made to accommodate three people comfortably, or a fourth person as well, by bunching up a mite, so Lige took his tin plate of stringy stew and bread to sop up the grease with, over nearer the door, and squatted Indian-like to eat his breakfast.

Cort Lane came over and hunkered next to Lige, which gave more room to the others at the table. He said, 'Just as well, I reckon,' and chewed a moment before contemplating it. 'Just as well we didn't find your paw. Want some advice, Lige? Don't try to find him. Leave him go his way, and you strike out to make your way.'

Lige ate and swelled inwardly with fierce

resentment. 'You fellers are sure strong on giving advice,' he said, speaking out to an older man for only the second or third time in his entire life. 'I don't need you nor the marshal to tell me what to do. And I'll find him, you can count on that.' Lige arose across to the far wall, squatted and resumed eating, alone. Cort did not speak to him again, even after they had trooped to the barn to rig out and get astride.

Only Marshal Farley said anything, the first mile after they were heading down-country. He dropped back to ride stirrup with Lige, and said, 'They'll likely only keep you locked up down there for a few days, boy. I don't know what the hell I can do.' He looked over. 'How old are you?'

Lige fought down an urge to lie, to add on three or four years. 'Sixteen,' he replied.

Evidently Farley had surmised this to be about his age because he shook his head as he spoke again. 'Hell of a thing. Well, I could tell you a few things, but you wouldn't want to listen to them. I hope you make it, all the same.' Marshal Farley urged his horse up ahead, and on in the east that bluish, steeldust colouring came like a pale streak upon the rim of the farthest horizon.

Swain was no longer chained, and behind him, the leadrope made fast to Swain's saddlehorn, came a saddled animal, but wearing a halter and shank instead of a bridle. This animal had the canvas-wrapped carcass of the dead man from the shoeing-shed.

Cort cut loose from the others after a while and loped ahead until he became lost to Lige's view. What Lige wondered now, was where these men were going. If they were fifteen days on the trail of the Harrows, were they now going to continue on that trail?

The deputy called Al, whom Lige knew least of them all, made a smoke, lit it, tipped back his hat and looked around at the countryside where it was beginning to tilt southwards towards the greater, open country down around Lincoln. He said to no one in particular, 'Better land down below than back up there on the high plateau.'

Matt, riding on Swain's far side, had a comment to make about that. 'You can have it. I'll take the land up north.'

For Swain, the slow progress towards his ultimate fate, whatever that was, could not have been at all pleasant, but when Lige looked over, the outlaw did not seem any different than he had when they'd been alone in the shed. Lige pondered that, trying to probe the depths of it. He did not know anything about fatalism, if that was indeed what held Swain impassively in his saddle, and he did not have much of an opportunity to speculate on it because Cort appeared, down-country a short distance, loping back.

Everyone watched the oncoming rider

without speaking, Marshal Farley stopped his mount, and raised a hand for those farther back to do likewise, then they all sat waiting.

Cort was wearing a blanket-lined, worn old denim rider's jacket buttoned part way up against the morning chill. He looked much older in the watery first-light, or maybe it was that he hadn't got much rest the night before, hadn't shaved nor even eaten very well, that made him look older.

He pulled up in front of Ben Farley, his hatbrim tugged low, even with the rock-hard eyes beneath the brim. 'Riders coming, Ben,' he said shortly. 'Looks like maybe eight or ten of them.'

Farley accepted that almost as though it were expected. He looked right, then left, and without a word turned his horse and squeezed it in the last direction he had looked easterly. There were some trees over there, the land was more broken and fissured with erosion gulches. The only person who seemed to derive fresh life from this latest development was Jim Swain. He stood in his stirrups to probe the onward gloom. Lige looked too, but the visibility was too poor, he saw nothing. He did not even hear anything, as his horse lifted its head and went hiking along behind the marshal and his deputies.

Swain glanced at Lige, made a merciless smile, and winked. That was all. Lige had no idea what it meant. If those oncoming horsemen were from Lincoln, then Swain had nothing to smile about, unless that smile had been an I-told-you-so smirk, because it would more-likely be a party of possemen.

He did not know the lawman at Lincoln. All he knew was that the man's name was Royce, Jack Royce. He had heard it a few times from his father, but that was all he'd heard, so he had no way of knowing what kind of a man Royce might be. He let his horse amble along until the broken country, with its scattered pines and firs, loomed dead ahead, then he raised his reins to check the animal up if Farley halted again, but this time Farley did not send anyone ahead to scout, he simply plunged dead ahead into the first arroyo, up the far side, and off into some trees that grew in a semi-circle upon the far rim of the arroyo. Then, finally, he turned to make certain everyone else was across, and raised his arm for another halt.

No one spoke as they sat motionless, all six of them. Lige heard nothing, at least for several minutes, but eventually he could detect shod hooves striking down over stones and gravelly earth. It sounded like a small army. He could tell the possemen were riding bunched up.

It only occurred to him when he saw Cort, Al and Matt, reach to loosen their sixgun tie-downs, that something was not right here. If those were possemen from town, then Marshal Farley should be glad to see them. But maybe

Ben Farley wasn't all that certain they *were* possemen, or maybe—

Ben Farley said 'Not a sound. Dismount and stand to your horse's head. Keep a hand to your horse's nostrils. Pinch off any nicker, and don't so much as scrape your boots. Swain—mind me now, because you're going first if they come over here.'

Lige swung off and moved up to lay a hand upon his mount's velvety muzzle. So did the others. The only man still upon a horse was the corpse.

The light was coming, finally, but it was like foggy well-water in the bottom of a jar. It was obscure and weak and filmy. Only against the eastern horizon was it actually clear, and turning rosy coloured.

The riders far ahead were slow-walking their mounts, and the sounds of spurs, rein-chains, and leather rubbing over leather, came softly.

Lige could not see those men up ahead. The sound told him nothing he had not already surmised. The possemen, if that is what they were, and he felt confident of that, were heading directly on a course that would take them to the Wyatt homestead.

He looked at Al, thinking it had been Al who must have alerted the marshal down in Lincoln. But why, if this were so, didn't these federal officers ride out and greet the possemen?

He gave up trying to puzzle it out, and stood

close as his horse suddenly raised its head, ears pointing forward. He settled his cupped hand to pinch off a nicker, but the horse made no attempt to call to the animals whose scent it had picked up. It was simply curious; not anxious to meet the other animals.

Cort swore softly. His horse threw its head, partly to be free of the hand upon its nostrils, partly because its curiosity about the horse-scent it was picking up, had agitated it. This animal was young. He had also been rested and well fed since the previous evening and was prepared for a new day with a full measure of spirit. Cort got the animal's head back down and put his hand upon the beast's nostrils again.

The horsemen passed, slowly but steadily, northward. They were quietly talking among themselves, the voices deep and masculine, the words blurred in the heavy gloom of pre-dawn.

Then they were gone and Marshal Farley worried off a chew of cut plug, spat grandly, toed in and rose up over his saddle. 'Let's move along,' he said. That was all there was to it. Lige did as he was ordered, but it loomed larger than ever in his mind that the U.S. lawmen had not wanted to meet the Lincoln posse. He worried about it as they struck out southward again, but this time through rougher terrain, and when Cort came up even, Lige said, 'That was the marshal from town, wasn't it? Why didn't you fellers just ride out to him and save him the ride back to the claim?'

Cort, who hadn't spoken to Lige since leaving the homestead, looked from beneath his lowered hatbrim and answered curtly. 'Town marshals and town posses aren't the best folks to meet when you have a murderer along.' Cort pointed to a stout fir limb growing about twenty feet off the ground and sticking straight out. 'And if there wasn't any constable along, boy, you see that limb up there? Well; maybe you'd be too young for it, but Swain isn't. They'd have saved the courts the cost of a trial.' Cort dropped his hand to the saddlehorn. 'In this line of work you don't ever want to lose a prisoner, and you don't want to get into any gunfighting brawls with cowmen-posses, if you can help it.'

CHAPTER TEN

THE SUBSTANCE OF FEAR!

The light did not change very swiftly, which was a little unusual this time of year. Usually, when a summer morning arrived, it came with a brilliant dazzle of golden light, as though someone Up There had tipped over a great cauldron to let the moulten brilliance gush downwards and outward, over all the uplands and the lowlands.

The reason this did not happen now, was not clear until Farley had led his riders out of the trees, on their southward route, and Lige made an instinctive, although cursory, examination of the overhead sky. There was a filmy weight of rainclouds up there. Some time in the night they had stolen in silently, had merged, and now formed a solid, gloomy overcast.

It did not strike Lige that this was appropriate until he lowered his eyes and saw the way Jim Swain, the outlaw wanted for two murders, was gazing out upon the grey-bright, half-lighted creeping dawn. Then Lige shuddered in spite of himself. Swain was going to lose, no matter how all this ended. Cort had thought Swain might lose back there where they had eluded the possemen. He would still lose, by his own admission, if they reached Lincoln without trouble.

They had left the trees, and the broken country, to start across the lowland range when Lige glanced back, for no reason, really, except that he was usually alive to feelings, to cross-currents, to all the vague layers and auras this time of morning, and saw the horseman sitting just clear of the trees, watching.

At first, Lige said nothing. He turned again, when they had progressed another hundred or so yards. That first time, in this poor and deceptive light, with the rider being backgrounded by the trees, and sitting perfectly still, he could have been a fantasy, an illusion. But the second time when Lige looked, the rider had loped ahead another few dozen yards, and was just reining up when Lige twisted the second time.

The only thing he could make out was the stranger was either trailing them, or had accidentally discovered them, and for whatever reason, did not want to ride up or try to skirt around them, and yet he was keeping pace behind them.

Lige straightened forward, looked at his companions, saw that each man around him was looking far ahead where what looked like a dark set of ugly squares hovered low upon the grey-lighted range, and turned one more time. The horseman was moving out again, hoping to close the distance a bit more, then he turned off and dropped down into a gully, quite disappearing.

Lige had had old wolves do that when he'd been out riding, out hunting. They would trail him, and when they saw him look back, they would either stop dead-still, or they would try to blend with their background. They did not harm mounted men; maybe, if a man or his horse became crippled they would attack, but that was a very remote possibility. Still, it had always made the hair along the back of Lige's head stiffen, and this same thing happened now, when the distant horseman faded from sight in the gloom back there.

He urged his horse up beside Cort Lane. 'That's the town up ahead,' he volunteered, and Cort looked at him.

'I can see it is, boy.'

Lige looked straight at the older man. 'You better pick up the gait so's we reach it soon.'

Cort's brows rippled together slightly. 'You in all that big a hurry, boy?'

'No, I'm not, but maybe you'd ought to be. There's a feller trailing us. He's been trailing us the last mile or so. If he was friendly, I figure he'd have ridden on up.'

Cort hauled back on his reins and twisted quickly in the saddle. Lige looked back too, but without halting his horse. The ghostly rider was not in sight. Cort let the others move along a few yards before abandoning his vigil and hurrying up again. He leaned and looked closely at Lige. 'You sure?'

Lige was very sure. 'Yes sir. He came out of the trees only a little while after we did.'

Cort hooked his horse and loped up to ride stirrup with Ben Farley. For a while they talked together, then Farley raised his arm and everyone drew rein. Farley turned, with Cort, and put a long, intent study upon the back-trail. The horseman was not visible back there. Lige looked too, and did not see him either. He was certain the pair of lawmen would think he had lied, and that was humiliating. But he *hadn't* lied, so he was adamant when Farley finally started onward again, leading them towards the dark, squatty blocks, onward through the overcast, and Cort let them all pass until Lige came up, then Cort swung in and rode beside him, studying the youth with a suspicious, unfriendly expression. Lige blushed, but it was not visible in the bad light. Then in his own defence he said, 'I saw him, and I don't care whether you'n Marshal Farley saw him or not.'

Cort said, 'I didn't say you didn't see him, boy.'

Lige, with defiance in him, was left hanging in limbo; expecting to be scorned, he hadn't been.

Cort looked back, then settled forward again. 'But just one man... Tell me, Lige, you'd ought to recognize your paw on a horse, hadn't you?'

It hadn't been his father. He knew that without knowing *how* he knew it. 'A stranger to me,' he replied. 'It wasn't paw.'

'You're sure of that?'

'Yes I'm sure. Only I couldn't see him too well when the trees was behind him.'

Cort looked back again, then fell silent and slouched along making a cigarette. When he had it lit he looked rearward one more time, but after that Cort seemed to accept the fact that whoever that had been back there, by himself there wasn't a damned thing he could do, if he had in mind freeing Swain or taking Lige away from the lawmen. 'Some rangerider full of curiosity,' he murmured, and inhaled then exhaled.

Lige did not believe it. 'It's awful early in the morning for riders to be out, and this time of year even down here on the grasslands, they don't have to do much riding.'

Cort considered this, then he smiled at Lige. 'Sometimes you talk like a grown man,' he said, which was flattering. *Particularly* flattering coming from this seasoned, hard man. Lige had no more to say, he savoured the compliment for a while, then, ahead, swinging out across the rangeland between the marshal's party and the distant town, a number of vague, blurry, mounted shapes materialized from the east and west, converging. Lige's breath caught up in his chest. He reached, touched Cort's arm, then pointed. This was another of those times, lately, when Lige's voice failed him through sheer fear.

Farley saw the materializing horsemen at about this same time, and hauled back so suddenly his horse snorted. They all stopped, bunching up. The lead-horse, half-asleep, bumped Swain's mount, and got roundly cursed for his clumsiness by the outlaw. That was the only sound for the moment or two. Cort rode up beside Marshal Farley. His words carried back where Lige was sitting.

'The damned possemen, Ben. I don't know how they did it, in this lousy light, but somehow they've gone and picked up our trail comin' down this morning. I thought we'd lost 'em back there.'

Ben Farley growled. 'Well, think again, damn it. How many do you make out?'

'Eight. And I don't like this, Ben. They're letting us come down to them. Sure as hell they're going to do a lynching.'

Farley's bronzed face congealed with rough resolve. 'Maybe. But if they do they're sure as hell going to know they've been somewhere.'

Neither Matt nor Al had a word to offer. Jim Swain rolled a cigarette as though this talking of hangropes did not concern him. Lige saw his steady hand hold up the light, and marvelled at the man's raw strength of character. It crossed his mind that a man such as Jim Swain knew, sooner or later, he was going to die like this; knew it, counted on it, and had been able to accept it for so long, that now, he really was not afraid.

It was, however, a very hard thought to accept and accredit for a youth of sixteen years. Lige may have been propelled into early manhood, and he may have acquitted himself, thus far at any rate, well enough as a newly matured individual, but he was still a boy in many ways, and the fear and dread of death that lingered from childhood was strong in him now. He could see a man like the outlaw sitting there, smoking, narrowly eyeing those strung out possemen downcountry, and be awed by Swain's silent, impassive acceptance, even disdain.

Marshal Farley spat amber down the off-side of his horse, and resumed his study of the possemen up ahead in the dismal light. 'They aren't making it look like they're very friendly,' he said to Cort Lane. 'I'll mosey up and talk a little with them. Cort, if I tip down my hat, you bust out of here towards the east, and if you got to, empty a few saddles, but get those two down to town. You understand?'

Cort understood. 'Yeah. Just once I'd like to ride into a strange country where they don't figure U.S. lawmen are as bad as outlaws.'

Farley lifted his bright, iron-like eyes, and smiled. 'What for? That'd take all the adventure out of this business.'

Cort snarled his comment to that. 'Adventure my tail!'

Marshal Farley urged his horse out at a slogging little walk, and when he'd gone about half way, he raised his hand in a salute to the strung-out riders. Not a one of them saluted him back. Lige had begun to feel the damp chill moments earlier, but now he was not conscious of it at all. He sat, fascinated and fearful.

Finally, Marshal Farley got down where those riders were. Several of them bunched around him, but if Cort had hoped the others, the farthest riders, would also converge, leaving his

91

route open in the direction of town, he got a disappointment. Three horsemen still sat out there, towards the east.

Al and Matt wheeled and positioned themselves upon both sides of Jim Swain. It was evidently an automatic thing, something they had learned to do over their years as manhunters. Swain looked first at one, then at the other, and pulled back his bloodless upperlip as he said, 'That's not real clever is it? If there's fireworks you boys can't protect me, and you could get shot right out of your saddles for being too close to me.'

Matt did not even turn when he said, 'Shut up!'

Lige looked sharply at Swain, but the outlaw was as calm as before, smoking, watching Marshal Farley down there arguing. He probably was accustomed to being spoken to like that by lawmen—perhaps by everyone.

Cort turned and looked at Swain too, then settled forward, dropped his right hand to tug loose the tiedown on his Colt, and to also remove his gloves, which he stuffed into his waistband behind his belt buckle.

They were tensely waiting for Ben Farley to reach and tug his hat forward, but it didn't happen. Farley finished his talk and turned, riding back. It reminded Lige of how his father had related palavering with redskins on the plains crossing. First, there was a council, then they were passed because there had been too many wagons in their train and too few Indians to really make serious trouble, or else because they had to cut out several horses for tribute, and buy their way past.

But this was different. From the slouched way Marshal Farley was returning, Lige had a sinking feeling that they weren't going to be able to buy their way past.

Cort rode ahead a dozen yards. He and Ben Farley paused to talk, out of earshot of the others, then they came back together. Cort looked as grim as Ben Farley did by the time they reached the others.

Swain spoke, looking bitterly amused. 'Hand me over and ride on, Marshal,' he said.

Farley only passingly glanced at him. 'You damned fool, I'd give you to them if I could, to make the trade, but they don't want you. Not even when I told them who you were and that maybe there's money on your head.' Marshal Farley jutted his chin. 'They want the boy.'

Even Swain was astonished. 'The kid?'

'Yes, the kid. They had some pretty well-thought of citizens shot a week or so back by an outlaw the kid's pappy re-outfitted. They've been scouring the country for the kid's father. They haven't even picked up a good lead. So they were heading up there to get the kid.'

Lige's mouth was as dry as dust. The fear was so strong now, as he listened to Ben Farley, and looked past at those eight men waiting to lynch him, he could hardly draw a shallow breath.

CHAPTER ELEVEN

CAPTURED!

Jim Swain said, 'For Chriz'sake, what kind of tomfoolishness is that!'

Cort answered. 'It's eight-to-four tomfoolishness, that's what kind it is. Two guns to one. Plus something else; we are strangers, and this happens to be their country. And one more thing; they are cowmen, and townsmen who make a living off cowmen, and the kid's a damned homesteader. Swain, you need anything more?'

The outlaw tossed aside his cigarette. 'Sure. If you're going to hand the kid over, you're a bunch of yellow bastards.'

Farley interrupted. 'Shut up, the both of you.'

Cort obeyed but the outlaw didn't. 'Hey, Marshal. Hand me m'Colt and arm the kid, then let's see how red-necked and tough them cowboys are. In my experience there's nothing with a smaller brain and a bigger mouth than a cowboy, and if he's from Texas, that goes twice over.'

94

Lige listened, and once the shock passed, he considered something his companions had not considered; flight. He had a very good horse under him, his own special horse. Maybe those stockmen down there could catch him, but he was sure of two things, only one or two of the horses down there would have the speed and the endurance, and the other thing was that he felt confident the moment the possemen started after him, Marshal Farley's party would start after *them*.

Matt, who hadn't said a word up to now, asked Marshal Farley a question. 'Are they really figuring on hanging the lad?'

Farley scowled. 'All they said was that they aim to take him to town and make him stand trial.'

Swain laughed. 'Some trial! It'll be held long before they get back to town—under a tree.'

It was easy for the others to make a swift judgement, they did not have to consider anything beyond that, but Ben Farley had a lot more to consider. For one thing, he was personally responsible for the deputies under him. For another, he was responsible for his prisoners, and for keeping the peace. He could not attack a posse of townsmen, even if they did not have a lawman leading them, even if they were simply an aroused group of irrationally angry citizens. But neither could he ever satisfactorily explain to his superiors that he had handed a lad of sixteen, who actually wasn't under arrest, over to a mob to be lynched.

In the end, Farley said, 'Cort, Al, Matt; pay attention now. I'm going down to palaver again. I'm going to try and get a couple of those boys to ride back up here and listen to what Lige has to say.'

Swain's eyes brightened sardonically. 'Then you're going to disarm 'em and hold 'em hostage. Marshal, you are wasting your time packing that silly badge, you ought to take to robbin' coaches and banks.'

Farley flared out. 'You shut your lousy mouth!'

Swain said no more.

Lige was torn between fear and resentment. He did not want those lawmen protecting him, in a sense, although he was enormously relieved that they were with him. He was also deathly afraid of those stockmen down there, waiting. He had never felt any liking for cowmen, a natural feeling among all immigrants, and their sons and daughters. He could not really say altogether *what* he felt; fear, resentment, dread, self-pity. It all added up to confusion, perhaps, but whatever the sum of it was, Lige sat still and silent while the older men made their plans.

Then, when Marshal Farley rode southward the second time, Jim Swain wagged his head and said, 'Boy, there's no way for this to turn out good.'

Cort put a black look upon the outlaw. 'You heard what the Marshal said, Swain; shut your lousy mouth!'

Swain did not have so much to lose he couldn't run the risk of Cort Lane's displeasure, so he spoke again. 'Give the kid a couple of guns. He's got a better horse than any of us, or any of *them*. At least that way he's got a chance, deputy. This way...' Swain shook his head slowly and adamantly.

Lige, having had this same idea, looked over to see if Cort thought much of it. Evidently Cort didn't, because he turned away ignoring the outlaw completely, and putting his full attention upon Marshal Farley, who was slightly more than half way down to the line of waiting possemen.

Farley slackened pace as a couple of those townsmen and stockmen rode out to meet him. Cort, watching as intently as were his companions, breathed a soft statement; 'By gawd I think he's going to be able to do it.'

But he didn't do it. The pair of possemen sat their horses, willing to talk, but evidently unwilling to ride up among the men Farley had left behind. They would have had to have been very naïve to do that, and apparently they weren't naïve; at least they did not seem *that* naïve.

Swain said, 'I told you it wouldn't work.' No one paid the slightest attention to Swain, whose garrulousness, now that there was a crisis, contrasted noticeably to his otherwise reticent attitude.

Something happened down there, though. The pair of possemen flagged their companions in with upraised arms, and Marshal Farley turned to ride back again. To Lige, whose hopes arose each time something occurred, because he wanted to believe he would survive this bizarre affair, it seemed that perhaps Marshal Farley had convinced the possemen to withdraw. At least, for the first time, they were all coming together, down there, and that *could* mean they were going to depart.

Ben Farley destroyed that thought when he got back up where Lige and Cort and the others waited. 'They wouldn't come,' he announced. 'But they had a plan to suggest. They'll escort us on down to Lincoln and see the lad and Jim Swain locked up for trial.'

Cort saw the flaw in this at once. 'Ben, that's *their* town. Once they get the kid in their jail, they'll just build up a bigger mob, then haul him out for a lynching. Swain too, more-likely.'

Marshal Farley looked steadily at Cort. 'There is no other way. We've got to play for time and send for help while we're guarding the kid and Swain in their damned town. We've got to get as much time as we can. The alternative is a gunfight here and now, with maybe more'r the kid and Swain getting killed.' Farley gestured. 'Look around you; there isn't a blade of grass out here for a man to get behind when he shoots. And remember, Cort, it's still two guns to one.'

There was a lot more involved than Marshal Farley mentioned. He, individually, could not let it come to a gunfight if he could possibly prevent that from happening. This alternative was not his idea of a good option, either, but as he had said, the only other choice was a fight. *That* had to be avoided, unless of course the possemen attacked, then Marshal Farley would be thoroughly justified in retaliation. Maybe only Cort understood fully. Lige didn't, and it was problematical whether the other two deputy marshals did either. Swain just plain did not give a damn.

Ben Farley avoided Lige's stare as he turned his horse to face southward. Down there, the possemen were waiting, evidently having completed their discussion. It was not hard to imagine the sly, knowing expressions on their faces. They had come out to get Henry Wyatt's son as an accomplice, and they were going to succeed, even though they also acquired four federal lawmen and a wanted killer in the same bag.

Without looking back Marshal Farley said, 'No arguing. Don't a one of you lay a hand upon a gun. Ride along and keep quiet. Cort; the minute we get down there, find the telegraph office and wire Denver to put some men on the next train out here. Explain what we're up against. Ask for at least four more deputies. Al, Matt; you boys don't go near any saloon in Lincoln. Stay close to the jailhouse—and be damned careful.'

Matt said, 'What in hell is their town marshal up to letting something like this happen?'

Farley snorted. 'Their town marshal belongs to the cowmen and the townsmen; they elected him, and their tax money pays his wages. That answer you? Town marshals are only supposed to protect the interest of their towns.' Finally, Marshal Farley turned his head. 'Lige; if you're scairt stiff, I can't blame you, but we'll do everything that can be done to keep your neck out of their damned rope. Now let's go.'

They rode ahead, walking their horses. It was a dangerous moment; all the lawmen were armed, all of them were tough, more or less fearless men. Waiting on both sides as the little party rode down country, were the cowmen and townsmen, also armed, and evidently just as determined.

Lige stayed beside Cort Lane, his feelings of independence and manhood dwindling with each step, until the possemen turned in on both sides and joined them on the southward ride.

Lincoln was not too much farther ahead, a couple of miles or less, according to Lige's calculations. The day, which should have been

100

bright and dazzling, continued dismal and overcast with a metallic scent to the air.

Lige recognized several of the possemen, but he did not see anyone he knew well enough to speak to, even if he'd felt like speaking.

No one said anything for a long while. Both parties were wary and watchful of the other, but Farley's men had their instructions and scrupulously obeyed them. This may have inspired the possemen to relax a little, but in any case, when Lincoln was dead ahead and not more than a half mile onward, a man Lige recognized as being the town blacksmith, a large, black-bearded, very massive man, turned towards Marshal Farley and said, 'How much reward did you say was on this Swain-feller's scalp?'

Farley's reply was short. 'I didn't say. I simply said there *was* a price on him. Without wiring our regional headquarters down in Denver, I wouldn't have any idea.'

Swain, the topic of discussion, rode along as slouched and easy as ever, casting a sardonic dark gaze upon the possemen from time to time. Evidently, Jim Swain did not differentiate between possemen with no more authority to enforce the law than they carried on their hips and their saddle-swells, and lawmen who had a legal license to kill and apprehend. Maybe he wasn't too far wrong in that respect.

A man Lige recognized as the clerk at the

general store, a little older than the others, craggy-faced with small, vindictive eyes, leaned and said, 'Boy; you can save your neck by tellin' us where your paw is.'

Cort turned. 'Leave the lad alone,' he growled, and the clerk hauled up stiffly in his saddle, glaring, but he said no more, and none of the other nearby possemen took it up.

They reached Lincoln with a soggy wind beginning to ruffle roadway dust and make the wash hanging out back of houses on clotheslines, whip and snap. It was one of those warm winds that presaged rainfall.

The town was quiet with very little noticeable activity in the roadway. People probably were anticipating the rain, and were preparing for it indoors. At the saloon, where several horses stood out front, three men came forth to stand silently upon the plankwalk and watch the mounted cavalcade pass along in the direction of the jailhouse. No one said anything to those men, from among the possemen, although there was a little head-nodding back and forth.

When they reached the jailhouse and turned in, the wind was beginning to gather potency. Three men from the liverybarn across the road came over, cursing and yanking their hats down hard to keep them from being blown off, to get the horses. Marshal Farley said he wanted his animals kept separate, and he wanted each one to be grained, curried hard, and fed plenty of hay. The possemen were a lot less explicit, probably because most of them would retrieve their mounts shortly, after they had seen the Wyatt boy and Jim Swain locked up, and head for whichever ranch they worked for, or perhaps for some shed in town.

Lige dismounted, had his horse taken from him, and when he looked at the man beside him, it was Cort Lane, already craning his neck to carry out those earlier instructions from Marshal Farley. Lige had ridden all the way into town thinking how pointless those instructions had been. Now, he leaned and tapped Deputy Marshal Lane on the arm.

'There isn't any telegraph office in Lincoln.'

Lige turned when someone poked at him, steering him towards the Marshal's office and the jail cells beyond. For some reason, Lige was nowhere nearly as frightened as he had been. Perhaps Swain's influence was prevailing, but more probably, since fear was not altogether self-sustaining, Lige had just been fearful for so long that he had worn it out.

CHAPTER TWELVE

JAILED

Jack Royce, the constable of Lincoln, stood in his little cell-room with U.S. Marshal Ben Farley and said, 'All right, Marshal, they didn't have the authority, but what harm did they do to you fellers? All they did was make plumb certain you got here with your prisoners.'

'Priso*ner*, Constable, not priso*ners*. The lad isn't under arrest.'

'He is here in this town,' exclaimed Constable Royce, a large, dark-haired, grey-eyed man in his mid thirties or early forties.

'What charge?' challenged Farley.

'Well; complicity, I reckon,' replied the local lawman, his broad back to the cell where Lige was locked in. 'He helped his paw.'

Farley said, 'I expect you'll have proof of that, Mr Royce?'

The constable's face began to darken. 'Whose side you on, Marshal? We had a bad robbery and gunfight down here couple weeks back, and before the outlaw died, we found out where he got his fresh animal and his directions for New Mexico. From Henry Wyatt.'

Farley grinned mirthlessly. 'From *Henry* Wyatt. Not from *Lige* Wyatt.'

'The boy knew what was—'

'You can prove that too, Constable?'

Jack Royce suddenly closed his mouth and stood, thumbs hooked, staring steadily at Marshal Farley. Then, without a word, he turned on his heel and stalked back out into his front office. From the strapsteel cage next to Lige's cell, Jim Swain laughed at Farley.

'Marshal; you'd ought to have known better. Now you've got him mad at you, and that means you'll not find out another thing—not even whether they'll be comin' tonight or tomorrow night, to hang me'n the lad. Marshal; you just got the whole damned town on you.'

It began to rain. Not very heavily, at first. For an hour and a half there was just a warm, pleasant drizzle that everyone welcomed because it settled the dust, cleansed the air, watered the rangelands, and made the world smell pleasant.

But in a place like Lincoln where all the roads and yards very quickly became quagmires of cloying mud-gumbo, it only required a couple of hours of rainfall to start people wondering when it would stop.

To Lige in his little twelve-by-twelve strap-steel cage, the rainfall was remote, even though he could hear it hammering overhead upon the jailhouse roof. Swain smoked and lay upon his wall-bunk, hat tipped down over his eyes, not asleep but thoroughly relaxed. After a while he lifted the hat, looked over, then said, 'What did you expect, kid? Your paw's got his own hide to think about.' Swain was quiet for a moment, studying the youth, then he spoke again. 'Don't stew about it too much. I can tell you for a fact the longer they delay busting in here, the more folks will commence arguing against it. Especially for you—you're only a kid. Big as a man, and all, but still only a kid. I looked at that meeting out yonder different than Farley did. I looked at it like this: If they brang us here and locked us in, and got to talking about lynching . . . Kid; there are too many womenfolk in a town like this. As soon as they get a drift of what's afoot . . .' Swain rolled his head from side to side. 'They'll never let 'em do it.'

The rain was increasing. Lige knew it was past midday, but not from the sky or the sunshine, just from calculating how long it had taken them to get to Lincoln.

Constable Royce brought them two bowls of some kind of meat stew. It could have been almost anything; cow, elk, buffalo, antelope, deer; neither Lige nor Swain commented because both were hungry. He also came back a second time with two tin cups of coffee. This time he leaned on Lige's cell and said, 'Boy; where is your pappy?'

Lige did not even look up. He went on spooning in the stew. Constable Royce's colour darkened. From the next stall Jim Swain said, 'He don't know. If he'd have known those federal marshals would have got it out of him. They tried. All he knows is that his paw was gone when the marshals caught him turning out a horse.'

Royce continued to lean, but now he studied Swain. 'I looked you up in my wanted file. There is four hundred dollars on you in Montana, and over in Nebraska. That makes eight hundred dollars.'

Swain sneered. 'I'd never have guessed you could add, Constable.'

Royce stiffened, but Swain did not drop his gaze. 'You're going to find out just how well I can add,' exclaimed Constable Royce, then turned back again to Lige. 'That dead man they brought in from your paw's claim, boy—what did his brother say while he was enjoying your folks's hospitality up there, where you run your outlaw camp?'

Lige knew Jack Royce only by sight, and at that, since he hadn't been to town a lot of times, he hadn't seen the town marshal very often. He knew almost nothing about Royce, but sitting inside a cell now, looking up at the large man, outside the cell, Lige decided that what had been said back up-country about the townsmen and the cowmen owning him, had to be right. That being so, then Royce was an enemy.

Lige said, 'That dead feller was dying. We

107

did all we could to help him. That's all I know about those two men, except that I didn't know they were outlaws. I stumbled on to them in some fog early in the morning. That's all.'

Royce said, 'Boy; you're lying to me. I've heard from at least a dozen people the last week or so, how you'd skulk around on the range for your paw, watching for the law and all.'

Lige's indignation erupted. 'That's a damned lie,' he exclaimed, and stood up facing the constable. They were about the same height, but right there was where all physical similarity ended.

From the next cell Jim Swain said, 'Set down, kid. Set down and don't let him get your goat. No matter what you tell a bastard like that, boy, he isn't going to believe it. He's already judged you and sentenced you. Don't waste your breath.'

Jack Royce threw a murderous look at Jim Swain. The outlaw still lay prone, cigarette drooping from his slit of a mouth, hat half-tipped forward above his eyes. Royce turned and stamped back out front, slammed the cell-room door, and Lige let the fighting stiffness drain out of him.

Something was happening to him that he vaguely understood was not a good thing; he was beginning to lean towards Swain's philosophy and Swain's outlook. He was beginning to want the company of a murderer, and no one had to be any older than Lige Wyatt was, to understand that this was a bad thing. He went to the barred rear slit of a window and leaned there, arms folded upon the worn-smooth stonework, looking out where puddles were forming and where the grey pall of a rainstorm was obscuring everything. If the sun had been shining, it would have helped, or if he could have seen the uplands to the north, he would have felt better. As it was, the jailhouse faced westerly, across the rangeland-country which was almost flat, and which ran for countless miles without a single high hill. It did not occur to Lige, but people raised near mountains, or reared in the hill country, never feel anything but exposed and unprotected in open country. The only thing he was certain of was that he was alone among people who did not like him, even though they did not know him. He was a homesteader; actually, the *son* of a homesteader, but in a cowtown like Lincoln that was no different than being the son of something else equally unflattering.

Cort Lane came in, later. Constable Royce would not allow either Lige Wyatt nor Jim Swain to have visitors unless he was present, so Cort handed the sack of Durham tobacco to Royce for examination, then pointed to Swain. Royce squeezed the little sack, then tossed it through the bars. Swain made no move to pick it up, although he did say, 'Obliged to you,

Deputy,' and ignored Constable Royce.

Cort studied Lige in silence for a moment, then said, 'You were right about there being no telegraph office.'

Lige felt no compulsion to comment on this from his position over by the slit of a barred window. He simply walked ahead to the bunk and sank down upon the edge of it.

'Marshal Farley's taking the evening stage down to Cheyenne where there *is* a telegraph office. He'll be back sometime tomorrow. Al, Matt and I'll hang around.'

None of this required anything from Lige, either, but he looked out at Deputy Lane, who was, in some ways, like Lige's father. He didn't waste words, he didn't seem to altogether like what he was doing, and he looked grave more often than he looked cheerful.

'You'll be all right,' Cort said. 'We'll be around, outside.'

Constable Royce shuffled to his feet impatiently and scowled at Deputy Lane. He was completely ignored by the federal peace officer.

Cort kept studying the lad through a moment of strained silence before saying anything more. Then he cleared his throat. 'We had a change in plans, Lige. We were going to keep on Harrow's trail. You knew that, because you heard us talking about it last night. Well ... Harrow is dead.'

This surprised Lige, who had been certain that, with the fresh horse and the long lead he'd had, the outlaw with the ivory-handled Colt and the stiff-brimmed hat would surely have been well along on the escape route. He said, 'Dead . . . ?'

'Yeah. He tried to stop a coach about sixty miles south of here.'

Constable Royce came into the conversation with some harshly-stated particulars. 'He *did* stop it. Only it wasn't a bullion coach, it was carrying some cowmen back home from a stockman's convention down near Laramie. They're going to bury him down at a little place called Shoshone. And boy, he was riding a horse fresh shod and sleek and strong, which he didn't get anywhere between here and there—so he got it from your place, which was the same place Deputy Lane here, and his friends, caught you turning out a worn-down horse.' Royce paused to allow Lige to digest this, then he said, 'You're into it up to your neck. Why don't you help us all by telling me the whole story?'

From the next cell Swain said, 'Why should he? You're going to hang him anyway so why should he give you any satisfaction?'

Royce turned swiftly and pointed a rigid finger. 'Mister, you keep it up, and you're not going to walk out of there—ever.'

Swain smiled. 'Hear that Deputy Marshal? He's just threatened my life. You'd better remember it, because your job's to protect—'

'Keep out of it,' exclaimed Cort, but without any particular rancour in his voice. 'Swain, you only make things worse for yourself, sounding off all the time. Just keep out of this.'

Swain scooped up the sack of tobacco and strolled to the rear of his cell to break it open and manufacture himself a cigarette.

Constable Royce was still furious, but without anyone left to vent his anger upon, he stood there with balled fists, saying nothing.

Cort sighed and shifted position with the appearance of a man who had more to say and who did not in the least want to say it.

Royce growled in a low voice. 'Tell him, will you? I got work to do.'

Lige heard, and sensed something. He raised his face.

Deputy U.S. Marshal Lane put out both hands and took hold of the cell's steel bars as he spoke again. 'I got some bad news for you, Lige . . . Your paw was killed on the southward trail. That's all we know so far, but it seems when he left the homestead yesterday he went hunting for Harrow. Maybe he figured Harrow would come back and help him to get you free. I don't know what happened. The rangeriders who found your paw said he'd been shot dead at pretty close range. My guess is that Harrow refused to come back and help, and maybe your paw meant to force him to, or something.

Anyway, there was one shot fired from your paw's pistol ... I hired a wagon from the liverybarn across the road to go down and fetch him back. I'm sorry ... Come on, Royce; let's get out of here and leave him alone.'

CHAPTER THIRTEEN

GUNSHOTS IN THE NIGHT!

The shock was so overwhelming that Lige did not have any urge to break down. It was also such an unbelievable thing, his father being dead. Over in the next cell Jim Swain was watching him from beneath his tugged-low hatbrim, and for once the outlaw had no comment to make.

Lige went back to the little slit-window, held the bars in his hands, and stared out where the rainfall was bringing on a premature darkness to the entire countryside.

Deputy Lane never would have said anything like that unless it were true. Moreover, just the *way* he had said it, *made* it true.

It didn't matter what his father was trying to do, seeking to get help from an outlaw to rescue Lige, and it no longer mattered what people in Lincoln thought of him, or what they wanted to do to him for their own tragedy in town a week

113

or so back. What mattered was that he *really was alone*, that his father was dead.

His mother was dead and now his father was dead.

An hour later, with the gloom thickening, Jack Royce entered his cell-room, hung a lighted lamp from a hook in the ceiling, hesitated a moment looking into Lige's cell, then went back out front again and barred the cell-room door. Swain returned to his bunk, covered his face with his hat, and slept. Later, when Jack Royce returned with two more bowls of the same meat stew, only Swain came alive long enough to eat. Lige had not moved from the window, did not seem to hear the constable's coming and going. Finally, Royce went out front where one of the deputy U.S. lawmen was always loitering, and said, 'The kid's taking it damned hard.'

It was the deputy called Al, who was standing watch this time. Al said; 'Well; wouldn't you?'

Royce closed the door and made a smoke and stood in the protection of the overhang watching rivulets form and shift and wash through one another as the rainfall kept up its monotonous cadence. 'Where's Lane?' he asked.

Al, who had taken an early dislike to the town marshal, replied in the same brusque way. 'Around somewhere. If you want him to talk to Lige, forget it. There aren't any words. There never are. If you've been through this as often as

114

we have, Constable, you'll just leave the lad alone.'

Royce inhaled deeply, then trickled out grey smoke. He turned to glance over across the roadway and northward, up where the lights of the saloon shone wetly. There were no horses tied out front, but that didn't mean there were no customers up there; in this kind of weather rangemen stabled their critters at the liverybarn. No one liked riding home astride a wet saddleseat.

Al yawned and cocked one foot up behind him against the front wall of the jailhouse. 'Been quite a bit of going and coming up there,' he said quietly, almost amiably, gazing in the same direction Royce was looking in. 'You don't reckon they're tanking up on Dutch courage for a lynching, do you, Constable?'

Royce flipped his cigarette. It arched into the downpour, then hissed itself to death before falling into the mud. 'There's not going to be any lynching,' he growled at Al.

'I'm right relieved to know that,' stated the deputy U.S. marshal. 'But you won't mind if I keep on hangin' around over here, will you?' Al's dark eyes glistened in the evening-shadows with cold irony. 'You'd be surprised how many men have been hauled out and strung up just because someone said it wouldn't happen, and someone else believed him.'

Constable Royce acted as though he had not

heard. He struck out through the mud for the plankwalk, then went hiking up it towards the saloon. Matt saw him pass from just inside the doorway of the livery barn. Cort also saw him pass, from up closer to the saloon, in the dark, recessed doorway of the gunsmith's shop.

The rain did not slacken even after full nightfall arrived. Lincoln showed lights almost everywhere except among the side-by-side stores and shops on both sides of Main Street, but after a while when the wind began blowing again, it seemed to sweep the downpour first one way then another way, but generally over against the buildings and not so much out in the centre of the roadway. Not that this mitigated anything very much. As far as Cort was concerned, in his recessed doorway, it would have been much better if the damned water had simply continued to come straight down, because now he caught an occasional wet veil even under the overhang, even back three feet from the exposed plank-walk.

He and his two companions had decided to keep this vigil after Ben Farley had departed on the evening coach. Farley hadn't given them any particular orders, except to make certain that no one lynched either Lige Wyatt, or their prisoner, Jim Swain. This had seemed to the deputies the surest way to make certain it didn't happen, even though all three of them were tired.

116

They also happened to be tough, inured men. This was not the first time they'd gone for a long while without rest, and unless they quit their current employment, it was unlikely to be the last time, either.

In fact, as Cort had said shortly before they had broken up to take their positions, right after eating supper in a hole-in-the-wall café, he could distinctly remember worse situations they had been in, on rainy nights, when there hadn't been any shelter at all. So this vigil was nothing so terrible they had to pity themselves.

Jack Royce emerged from the saloon, turned southward, and began a slow march down the eastside plankwalk. Cort peered out and saw him coming. He also noticed what Royce was doing; pausing at each doorway peering in.

Someone had noticed Cort in the gunshop doorway, and undoubtedly, up at the saloon, had passed along this scrap of information. Cort was not worried. When Royce finally came down and looked in, Cort said, 'Driest place I could find, Constable.'

Royce ignored this to frown. 'There is not going to be any trouble, Deputy.'

Cort nodded his head. 'You're damned right there isn't, Constable. Or, if there is, there isn't going to be any lynching. Not tonight. Not until Marshal Farley gets back. And not then, either.' Cort leaned comfortably in his little recessed place. 'How is the kid?'

'Standing by the back window looking out, the last time I was in there. Just standing holding to the bars, not making a sound.'

Cort said, 'You've got a nice town here, Constable. Must be full of nice people—so busy hating a kid they are acting like a bunch of coyotes skulking in a pack.' When Royce would have spoken, Cort raised a gloved hand. 'I heard the talk up there in the saloon, Constable.'

Royce looked down at his muddy boots for a moment. 'I told them—no trouble.'

Cort said, 'You told them the wrong thing, Constable. You should have told them the first man who tries to kick in that door over there, is going to die in his tracks. Folks understand that kind of talk a lot better than when someone tries to joke them out of being mean.'

Royce glared. 'I've got to live here, you don't.'

Cort accepted that. 'I understand. In fact, we figured you about right before we ever rode into your town. But it's not that easy, wearing the badge they voted you to have, Royce. A man has to live with something a lot more important than a lot of friends and acquaintances, no matter where he hangs his hat. He's got to live with his conscience.'

Up the roadway some men emerged from the saloon, all in a bunch. Cort raised his gloved hand to Royce's chest, and pushed. He said, 'Get out of the way, Constable.' His tone had

118

turned knife edged. Royce gave ground and Cort moved from his recessed doorway.

It looked like no more than three or four men, up there, and although it was possible that they had been drinking, they did not act drunk. One of them pointed down in the direction of Cort's recessed doorway, speaking to the others; even if he hadn't been too distant for his voice to carry, the drumroll sound of rain would have drowned him out, but Cort had no problem guessing his instructions. Whoever it was up there who had told Royce one of the U.S. marshals was standing in the gunshop doorway, had undoubtedly told others too.

A pair of burly shapes detached themselves from the gloom of the saloon's front wall and started walking southward.

Cort studied those two men a moment, then he turned and gestured. 'Constable; you'd better stop those two.'

Royce peered up the dark plankwalk. In a low and troubled voice he said, 'I don't know who they are.'

Cort turned on him, his tone cold. 'It don't matter who they are! You stop them or I will. They're coming down here to test me out. You know that as well as I do. Now, Constable, it either stops here and now, or someone's going to get hurt.'

Royce still procrastinated. 'I told them there wasn't to be any trouble.'

Cort stepped back two paces, until he was slightly behind Constable Royce, then he drew. It was the sound of the gun being cocked that brought Jack Royce to life. He sang out. 'Lem; Charley; go back! I told you—no trouble. Now, dammit, go back!'

One of those oncoming burly figures called to the town marshal. 'Where is he, Jack? Flush him out and we'll settle this.'

Royce was turning, his face twisted with anguish, when Cort fired the first shot. A plank no more than a foot ahead of the oncoming pair of men, flew apart as the slug struck it dead-centre. One of those men let out an astonished squawk. The other one crouched, and Cort fired higher the second time. For that man to crouch had been a very foolish thing; he was facing a drawn, cocked gun. When the bullet struck him, that crouched man's legs went out from under him, backwards, he fell hard upon the broken strip of plankwalk, then rolled off into the inches-deep mud of the roadway. He was gasping, trying very hard to keep from screaming. The second man had his hands to his shoulders. 'Hold it, hold it,' he cried out.

Constable Royce was rooted in place. Back up at the saloon men tumbled from inside to stand crowding up close out front as Cort called to the uninjured man. 'Get him out of the mud. Take him back to the saloon. The next man who walks down from up there isn't going to get a warning shot.' Cort nudged Constable Royce with his gun-barrel. 'Go help the damned fool. And Royce, you'd better convince them; you'd better explain to them that U.S. lawmen are as justified in killing to protect their prisoners as county sheriffs are. Go on.'

Royce went, lumbering awkwardly.

Cort stepped back to his doorway, plugged out the two spent casings, plugged in a pair of fresh loads from his shellbelt, holstered the gun, and leaned, watching Constable Royce and the other bulky man lift the injured one between them, and start staggering nothward under that rather considerable weight.

Then Cort left his doorway, went southward as far as the liverybarn where Matt was craning out to see everything, and explained what happened. Matt acted worried. 'That's likely to stir the whole passel of them up,' he exclaimed.

Cort agreed. 'Sure is. Come along. We're going to do the rest of our waiting inside the jailhouse. I don't like it, having them box us in like that, but we sure don't have any back-protection out here, even in the dark.'

They crossed over where Al, still with one leg cocked up against the front of the jailhouse greeted them with a thin grin. 'Where'd you hit him?' Al asked Cort.

'In the leg. At least I held it down that low.' Cort shrugged, and the three of them entered the jailhouse office where Royce had left a lamp

121

alight atop his desk.

Matt barred the door, went over and examined the rack of carbines and shotguns upon the far wall, then joined Al at the potbellied stove. They rummaged for the means for brewing some coffee. It was not very warm inside the jailhouse, either; not cold, exactly, just clammy-damp, so when the stove was lighted and the pot placed atop it, two needs were being served.

Cort made a cigarette, with his hat shoved back. Al suggested telling Swain and the kid what had happened, because they surely had heard the gunshots. Cort lit up, broke the match, and shook his head. 'Swain can guess and the kid doesn't want to talk to anyone. Let it go; maybe by morning we'll have more to tell.'

They put the lamp upon a peg hanging from the south wall so that it would not background them, then they slipped to the pair of barred front windows on either side of the barred door, and stood slouched, peering out. It was still raining, visibility was extremely poor, and if there was anyone out there they could not see him unless he moved. There was no movement so they decided after some casual conversation, that the man with the broken leg up at the saloon had probably exerted a restraining influence.

Matt looked at their inadvertent fort and made a sound observation. 'Thank the lord it's

122

raining; if some silly damned drunk took a notion to pitch a firebrand on to the roof of this place, we'd get cooked to a fare-thee-well.'

When the coffee was finally ready, they filled three tin cups from a shelf and made themselves comfortable. It was a poor night for heroics, what with the rain coming down in torrents and three obviously willing and capable U.S. lawmen holed up in Lincoln jailhouse. Cort did not expect any more trouble, but when he said this, Al and Matt simply sipped coffee and gazed sardonically at him, saying nothing.

CHAPTER FOURTEEN

CRISIS IN THE STORM!

The rain appeared to diminish after ten o'clock, or perhaps it was simply that the wind seemed to increase, making more noise than the downpour could make, but whatever it was, there did in fact seem to be a change coming in the weather.

The town stood cowed upon its sodden rangeland plateau, an occasional light braving the elements to throw a steady orange glow outward. Up at the saloon, there was also a fire popping in the big iron stove. Down at the jailhouse, although the stove was smaller, so was the room it had to heat, so the end result was identical in both places.

Jack Royce, in a long, sweeping raincoat, came ploughing back across the roadway to bang upon his office door, and be admitted. He shed water on the floor like he'd been completely immersed in the stuff. None of the lawmen offered him coffee even though the pot and cups, and even the coffee itself, belonged to him. Al and Matt were comfortably sprawled in chairs, with shotguns they'd appropriated from Royce's wall-rack, and Cort was standing wide-legged, back to the crackling stove.

Royce said, 'You broke that feller's leg above the knee,' to Cort. 'They're mad as hell about that.' He did not have to explain who 'they' were.

Deputy Lane drained the last of his coffee, then replied dryly, 'Maybe they'd be a lot madder if I'd killed that damned fool.' He put the cup aside. 'Just *how* mad are they?'

Royce shrugged out of his raincoat and draped it from a nail in the back of the streetside door, then he shed his hat and walked over to get some coffee. 'Mad enough,' he retorted, succinctly, and with his back to the federal lawmen he said, 'I talked a feller from the livery barn into coming around back with a horse for the kid. He's got to be taken out of here.' Royce turned, cup in hand, and looked steadily at Cort. 'You can go with him, if you'd like. There's several places around town where you can hide him until morning, when they've simmered down. Maybe by then the Marshal will be back and we won't have any more trouble. But for tonight...' Royce drank his coffee without finishing his suggestion.

Cort and the companions exchanged a look, then Matt spoke out. 'You mean they're going to try and storm this building?'

Royce did not know. At least he shrugged that question off as he replied. 'Maybe. There's a lot of them up there; townsmen and cowmen, and they've sent out for more. All I know is that if the kid isn't here, they aren't going to shoot anyone, or hang anyone, are they?'

Cort was thoughtful. 'And how about you? They're going to guess you had a hand in hiding the kid.'

Royce acknowledged that. 'I reckon,' he replied laconically. 'But they won't do anything to me. And they don't give a damn about Swain. It's just the kid they want.'

Al, who disliked Jack Royce, put a dark stare upon the constable. 'When did you have such a change of heart?'

Royce swore. 'Hell; I told you over and over I didn't want any trouble. That's what I'm concerned about. I don't want any more shooting, any more fighting. Someone's going to get killed, eventually... Just hide the kid, let them see that he isn't here, then let them puzzle over that until morning. Everything will look different come sunrise.'

Cort went to perch upon the edge of the desk. He did not particularly want trouble either. He was prepared for it, and he would certainly become involved in trouble if it came, but, like Marshal Farley, he would like to see it avoided if that could be done. 'When is this feller coming from the liverybarn?'

'Shortly,' Royce answered. 'He'll come to the rear door and knock three times. There will be two horses. He'll show you where to take the Wyatt kid, down near the lower end of town where there is an old granary. You'll be safer there than anywhere else.'

'How about the liveryman?' asked Al. 'What's to keep him from going up to those fellers in the saloon and selling Cort and the kid out?'

Royce, perhaps seeing success within reach, vehemently shook his head over this idea. 'Not Lefty; I use him for a deputy town marshal now and then. He's the most dependable man in town. He just got back about a half hour ago from picking up Henry Wyatt's body down along the south road.'

Cort was interested in this fresh development. 'Where's the body now, over at the liverybarn?'

'Yes. Still in the wagon, covered with blankets.'

'You saw it?'

126

Royce nodded. 'Yeah.' Then he returned to his original topic. 'And there's something else. Maybe this was inevitable, but with all the talk and excitement in town, some of the damned homesteaders scattered over the countryside are beginning to drift in—armed.'

Royce did not have to spell this out, the implication was clear enough. Cort got off the edge of the desk, went to a front window and looked out. The rainfall was dwindling down to a steady soft drizzle and most of the wind had died away. It was possible to see up the roadway a fair distance. The saloon seemed more lively now than it had been earlier. While he was standing there, Matt had a thought. 'Cort; if it comes to a head this is going to be one hell of a mess, us shooting at townsmen and cowmen, them shooting at us—and some damned homesteaders shooting at us both. Ben wouldn't like it at all.'

Cort turned back facing into the room. 'Go listen for the man with the horses, Matt. Al, fetch Lige out here.' As the other deputies arose to obey, Cort fixed Jack Royce with a sulphurous gaze. 'Constable, I sure hope this isn't a trick of yours to get the kid out of the jailhouse, because if it is . . .' Cort did not finish it, and Jack Royce spoke up too soon for Cort to say more if he'd meant to.

'All right, Deputy, if you want, I'll go along with you.' He did not deny it was a trick, he simply offered to help protect Lige Wyatt.

Cort considered that for a moment before speaking again. 'You were the one who insisted that the kid be arrested and held. Now, it's beginning to look as though you don't want him held.'

Royce swore in exasperation. 'You've got an ivory skull,' he snapped. 'What I *don't* want is a lot of people to get shot and maybe killed. Not over the Wyatts. Have you ever seen a riot hit a town, Deputy? I have, a couple of times, and I'd ten times rather see someone like Lige Wyatt get clean away, than to see people running through my town firing buildings and shooting at anything that moves. Take my word for it, Lane, those fellers at the saloon have been drinking steadily. When that man came back in with the broken leg, they were agitated enough to storm this lousy jailhouse. You understand what I *don't* want to see happen?'

Al returned from the cell room with Lige Wyatt. The youth was stony-faced as he glanced from Jack Royce to Deputy U.S. Marshal Cort Lane. He looked older, if that were possible, than he had looked seven or eight hours earlier, in the morning of this grey and threatening day.

Cort made a smoke and lit it without speaking. He was making a decision that actually wasn't his to make. Ben Farley was the one to decide something like this, but of course Farley wasn't there. Maybe what Cort was doing would turn out all wrong; if so, it would be Cort Lane's neck on the line. He inhaled, then said, 'Al; go back where Matt is. Take a long look at this damned liveryman. If anything at all makes you suspicious, slam the door and bar it.'

After Al departed Lane went over by the desk again. He looked at Lige, then at Jack Royce, then back to the youth again as he said, 'You're going out of here by the back alley. There's trouble coming.'

Lige spoke tonelessly. 'Give me a gun and I'll take my chances right here.'

Jack Royce swore again. 'Gawddammit, what's the matter with you, boy; you want me to end up dead too?'

Lige turned on the town constable. 'Give me a gun and find out,' he snarled.

Cort punched out his cigarette. 'That'll be all of that kind of talk,' he said. 'I know how you feel, Lige, but striking back like a blind rattler isn't going to help any.'

Al came through the rear office door. 'He's out there, Cort, and he looks all right.' Al glanced at Lige, then at Royce. 'And there's some kind of commotion starting up at the saloon.'

Cort stepped to a front window, stood gazing out for a moment, then turned and gestured. 'Out the back way, Lige.' He didn't give the youth a chance to speak or to cause any delay, he gave him a rough push. They all passed along to

129

the rear-alley doorway of the jailhouse. The drizzle was still falling, but it was the keening wind that made them all flinch, after having been inside where it was warm for several hours.

Royce would have come out into the muddy alleyway too, except that Cort growled at him. 'You stay here with Al and Matt. How would it look if *both* you and the kid were gone when those lynchers show up? And Royce, you'd better be able to talk them into their senses. If they hang Swain you're going to be in a whole lot of trouble.'

The liveryman was a thick shape inside a black raincoat with a crumpled old hat atop his head. Very little of his face was distinguishable, which was understandable in the biting cold.

Matt came out with Lige and told him to mount one of the horses. Al, watching all this, scratched his jaw with a puzzled expression; if Cort and the Wyatt kid were going no farther than the end of town, why did they need horses? It was one of those self-asked questions that very often did not survive ridicule when it was put into words, so Al simply scratched his jaw in bafflement and kept silent.

Lige turned towards Constable Royce. He seemed willing to say something, but in the end, when Matt gave him a shove to mount the horse the heavy-set liverybarn hostler was holding, Lige swung up. It wasn't the horse he'd ridden down from the uplands, but that didn't appear

130

to matter. Nothing seemed to matter a whole lot to Lige as he evened up his reins and looked round where Cort was standing, waiting, apparently, for Lige to be astride, and perhaps waiting for what someone might say, over by the back of the jailhouse. Then, finally, he mounted.

The liveryman did not have a horse but he struck out, swishing through mud in his trailing, shiny black raincoat looking more like a bear than a man. Royce and the pair of deputy U.S. lawmen at the jailhouse doorway watched only until they were confident everything was going properly, then they ducked back inside where the warmth was.

The wind began to diminish, which was not altogether reassuring because it had done this once before only to return with fresh vengeance sometime later. The drizzle, though, still fell unabated. Where a horse's hoof sank, then pulled free with a sucking sound, walls of mud instantly caved in on all sides obliterating every sign of the hoofprint. The buildings they passed were dark and wet-shiny.

Cort thought it was one hell of a night. He'd been out in other ones as bad, but never under quite these same circumstances. He had long ago developed the capacity to withdraw—to sort of detach himself from his surroundings, which was a very good trait to develop if a man lived as Cort Lane had been living for some years now since he'd taken the oath of office as a deputy U.S. Marshal.

He let the horse slog along, shaking its head from time to time as rainwater trickled into its ears; there were a lot of things horses did not like, but water in their ears was foremost.

Lige rode beside Cort, his jacket darkening under the rainfall, his head tipped down, his face a pale blur beneath his dripping hatbrim. If a person hadn't known better, he would have thought Lige Wyatt was about as old as Cort Lane was.

They passed down where the buildings were fewer and farther between. There were no lights at all, down here. Their guide, stumping along like an oversized gnome, led them to the very end of Lincoln, then out a few dozen yards, and halted, head cocked, but nothing short of a cannonshot would have been audible in this stormy night. Next, he stepped out and cast a searching look all around, which Cort seemed to think was unnecessarily melodramatic. Cort said, 'There's no one. Get on with it.'

The liveryman turned back, walked between the standing horses and pointed a cocked sixgun upwards. Cort was caught completely by surprise. So was Lige, but when the thick-set shape in the shiny old raincoat said, 'Reach over, son, and take his gun,' Lige threw up a hand in shock, or astonishment. He had recognized the voice. *It belonged to his father!*

132

CHAPTER FIFTEEN

A DEAD MAN WITH A GUN

U.S. Deputy Marshal Lane did not object when Lige Wyatt disarmed him, he sat there, hatbrim dripping rainwater, staring at the nearly concealed face of the man in the raincoat and sodden slouched hat.

Lige too, even though he had a gun shoved into his waistband, and had an overwhelming gush of fresh elation, sat his saddle staring at the man on foot, who gently lowered his sixgun, then shoved it somewhere beneath his raincoat as he said, 'Deputy, the last thing in the world I ever wanted was trouble with the federal law. But I got to get my boy out of here. Maybe you can protect him, but I'm his father, that's more my responsibility.'

Cort blew out a big breath, then spoke. 'I was told you got killed down south.'

Henry Wyatt said, 'That was Harrow, and a man he was riding with; someone he met along the trail. I don't know his name. All I know is that by the time I caught up with Harrow, this other feller was in his camp.'

Cort said, 'Dead?' and Henry Wyatt shook his head.

'He wasn't dead—then. I rode in to get

133

Harrow to come back up here with me and help me get Lige free. I offered Harrow a thousand dollars cash, but he said he wouldn't go back north, even as far as Lincoln, for ten times that much. But the other man said he would; then he got the drop on me and laughed when I told him I didn't have the thousand dollars on me, that it was cached back at my homestead. He was going to shoot me. Harrow killed him, then he told me if I kept following him he'd kill me too. Harrow left. He was bound for New Mexico.'

Cort said, 'He didn't make it, Mister Wyatt; he tried raiding a stage full of cowmen near some place called Shoshone, and they killed him.'

Obviously, this was fresh information to Henry Wyatt, because his jaw hung slack a moment. Then he recovered. 'Harrow don't matter anyhow,' he stated. 'Deputy, I got to take your horse.' Henry Wyatt looked genuinely anguished. 'I know—this is going to make you look bad; maybe cost you your job, but what would you do in my boots, if this was your son?'

Cort said, 'The same, I reckon,' and swung down to stand in the mud. 'I won't lose my job, Mister Wyatt, I'll get the assignment to hunt you and Lige down, though.' He tossed over the reins and reached up to button his rider's jacket at the throat to prevent water from seeping in. 'How in the hell did you get back here, like this?'

134

Henry Wyatt fidgetted in the soggy earth. 'I'm not going to tell you that, Deputy, except to say I bribed my way, and you know a feller who'd take money from me to let me impersonate him, would sell out to someone else the same way. That's why Lige and I've got to get to riding.'

'Who was it came back here as your corpse,' asked Cort, 'the feller Harrow shot when he tried to hold you up?'

Henry Wyatt nodded. 'Him.'

Cort had the answer to his earlier question now. He said, 'So the dead man came back in the wagon we sent southward to fetch back your carcass, which means that the liveryman or one of his hostlers, whoever drove that wagon, and who knew you by sight, knew damned well that *wasn't* you they loaded up and brought back.'

Henry Wyatt did not affirm this nor deny it, he simply motioned Cort out of the way, then stepped close and swung up over leather while Lige kept eyeing the deputy U.S. lawman, one hand resting lightly upon Cort's sixgun.

'Where did Jack Royce fit in?' asked Cort, and got a short answer.

'He didn't fit in at all. When he come to the liverybarn to have a pair of horses brought around back of the jailhouse, I was hiding in the loft and heard.'

Cort nodded. 'And you made another bribe.'

Henry Wyatt nodded. 'Yes sir.' Then he

leaned a little to speak again. 'Deputy, I don't justify what I done back up at the homestead, except to say that if I *hadn't* done it my wife and boy would have starved that second winter like they almost starved the first winter. There is no charity in this country, not for homesteaders. I couldn't do anything else; I never wanted to sell mounts to outlaws, but I wanted a lot less to see my family starve. It was wrong. I know that, and I always did know it. Now, we're heading for a new country and a new start. You got my word for it, Deputy, I'll never break the law like that again.'

Cort and the other older man looked steadily at one another for a moment, then Cort swung his attention to Lige. 'How about you, cowboy?'

Lige hadn't spoken until now. His voice had failed him, as it often did under extreme strain, when he'd first recognized his father, the man he'd wept inwardly for, half this bitter night, but now he experienced no difficulty when he said, 'I never went outside the law, Mister Lane. Well; not until the day you fellers came up. I never wanted to, and I never wanted my paw to have neither.'

Cort did not smile but he nodded a little. 'Good luck, Lige.'

'You'll be coming after us?' asked the youth, and Cort did not answer this nor alter his expression, he simply gestured for them to ride, and he repeated what he had already said.

136

'Good luck.'

Henry Wyatt led off. Lige kept looking at Deputy Lane until he was well past, then he settled forward and followed his father out into the soggy, gusty night. The pair of them were lost to sight within minutes. Even the strong, sucking sound of horses's hooves being pulled from the cloying mud a step at a time, was lost within moments.

Cort stood a moment or two, reflectively, then he turned eastward, crossed the lower end of the main roadway, found the back-alley upon the opposite side of the road, and went up as far as the lighted interior of the liverybarn. He walked in, up there, without encountering a soul, located the dingy little office, yanked back the door and stepped inside where a paunchy, unshaven man was sitting, booted feet cocked up, reading a limp old newspaper at a scarred desk. The man seemed to know who Deputy Lane was; his small, crafty eyes got perfectly round. Cort gazed dispassionately downward and held out his right hand.

'Do you own a sixgun?' he asked.

The hostler brought his feet down off the desk and tugged open a desk-drawer. There were three sixguns in there. Without a word Cort examined all three, selected the best one, dropped it into his holster, then stepped closer to the woodstove where the heat made his wet clothing steam, and said, 'Have you any idea

137

what aiding and abetting a fugitive from the law can net you in prison?'

The hostler sucked in air like a fish out of water. Weakly he said, 'Me?'

Cort nodded. 'I just came from a long talk with Henry Wyatt. He freed his kid and rode— northward.'

The Wyatts had ridden southward.

The hostler sniffled and dragged a soiled sleeve across under his nose, then he leaned to stand up, but Cort shook his head, so the paunchy man did not arise. 'All's I did,' he whined, 'was fetch back a corpse rolled into some old blankets and put it beside that dead one you fellers brought in earlier. How was I to know it wasn't Henry Wyatt?'

Cort's lips parted in a death's-head smile. 'You knew. You took money to help Henry Wyatt.'

'He held a gun on me,' bleated the fat man.

Cort's bloodless smile lingered. 'I'm sure he did. Mister, I'll give you some advice. Be fifty miles from Lincoln, come morning, and don't stop and look back, because when the U.S. Marshal returns, we're going to be on your trail.' Cort patted the gun. 'This evens up for the one the Wyatts took from me. At twelve dollars each, on my wages, I can't afford to just hand these things around.' Cort walked out of the stale-smelling little office, walked on up through the barn to the muddy roadway, and

138

hesitated a moment to look up and down the plankwalk before stepping off to head on across.

He felt, in his bones, that Jack Royce had known who that man was in the long black raincoat—Henry Wyatt. He thought he understood why Jack Royce had allowed this thing to happen, too, and perhaps, he told himself, in Royce's boots he would have done the same thing. But somewhere, the responsibility had to settle, and as he stood looking up and down the roadway, he decided it had to settle upon Constable Jack Royce.

Of course there was a problem there; Cort had no way under the sun to actually *prove* that Jack Royce had a hand in the escape of the Wyatts...

He would have stepped down into the mud, but across the way something bulky moved, gliding up from the north side of the jailhouse. Watery light glistened off blue steel.

Cort stood perfectly still, watching. Three more of them glided forward. They bunched up in their glittery black raincoats until it was difficult to tell one from the other, at the roadway, north corner of the building; they seemed to be in earnest conversation.

Cort turned his head left, then right, but he did not see any but those four. He moved swiftly away from the interior light of the liverybarn, faded into the soggy shadows on the north side, then flattened, waiting to see what those four men were up to.

They seemed either undecided or unwilling to settle upon a unanimous course of action. Two of them started along towards the front door of the jailhouse, and were angrily called back by the other two. They returned, reluctantly, and as Cort watched, one of those men swung his arm in some kind of gesture while the other three stood in the wind-driven drizzle. The man who gestured stood straighter than his companions. Cort had no idea who he was, and did not really care, as he drew the Colt he had acquired inside the liverybarn office, hefted it, found the balance satisfactory, and fired from the hip.

The bullet flung up a great gout of mud. Those four men across the road reacted more to the muzzle-blast and the explosion than they did to the mud. Two of them plunged back down the north side of the jailhouse, and a third one, hurling himself down there too, either slipped, or bumped one of the others, but in either case, he fell in a cursing heap. Cort saw his gun slip away and land out in the roadway, in a big puddle. It sank like a stone.

The fourth man, that large, erect one who had been trying to create order among his companions, threw up a gun. Cort could have dropped him in his tracks. The reason he didn't was because he knew that man over there could not discern him in the darkness and the downpour.

The man hesitated before firing, which would ordinarily have been fatal. Then he cut loose and the slug struck the front of the liverybarn over near the wide, doorless opening, as though the gunman across the way thought Cort had fired from inside the barn, then had perhaps ducked back.

Cort still held his fire, but from inside the jailhouse someone poked out a shotgun and let fly. That unmistakably lethal roar unnerved the gunman. He turned and fled down the north side of the jailhouse in the wake of his vanished friends.

Cort punched out the expended casing, put in a fresh one, holstered the gun and turned to look northward. Up at the saloon, where the lights were as bright as ever, several men stepped forth and foolishly stood limned in the glow coming forth over the top of the batwing doors. Cort shook his head; irate townsmen and cowmen, at least in Lincoln, didn't use the sense God gave a goose. Cort could have killed those men up there with three or four shots, and been in no peril himself at all.

But he did not even draw the gun. He allowed a couple more minutes go by, certain that it would take that long for the men he'd just routed to regain the saloon, then he ploughed ahead on across the roadway and struck the front door with his gun-barrel. 'It's me, Cort,' he called, and struck the door again, until it opened, then he stepped inside. Al and Matt stared. Jack Royce, with a shotgun in his hands, was reloading the weapon over by the stove. He also looked surprised. Cort wished he could be sure whether Royce was acting or not. If he *was* acting, then he was damned good at it.

Matt found his voice. 'What the hell— where's the kid?'

Cort said, 'Gone,' and stamped over to help himself to a cup of coffee. To Royce he said, 'You didn't hit any of them, but between us I think we scairt hell out of them.'

CHAPTER SIXTEEN

DAWN'S SOGGY ARRIVAL

Cort explained in a quiet tone of voice exactly what had happened at the south end of town, and as he did so he kept watching Jack Royce, something the constable had no trouble understanding. When Cort was finished, Royce put aside the scattergun and said, 'I didn't have a damn thing to do with it. But I'm glad he's gone; glad they're both gone. And in case you boys would like to know—I figured that band of horsemen might ride up to the Wyatt homestead. I told them not to do it, when they wanted me to go along. My authority ends at the town limits. Anyway, I sent a letter to Denver for some U.S. law to come in here and sift through whatever Henry Wyatt was up to.'

The U.S. lawmen looked interested. Cort said, 'How long ago did you send that letter?'

'Day before yesterday.'

The U.S. lawmen lost interest. It would take that letter probably until tomorrow just to reach Denver, and assuming someone was sent out, which was not altogether likely, they wouldn't arrive in Lincoln for about another week.

Someone came to the front of the building yelling for Constable Royce. Cort stepped to one side of a window and peeked out. It was just one man. He motioned for Royce to open the door, then he motioned for Al and Matt to get into position. When Royce lifted the bar and swung the door inward, a large, dripping-wet man entered the office. He removed his hat, looked at the guns aimed in his direction, and went over to back up close to the stove, before he said, 'Jack, I want to report a horse stole from my liverybarn tonight. And I know who stole it, too; that damned Lefty Turnbull, my night-hostler.'

Royce looked from the irate liveryman to the deputy marshals. 'This here is Richard Barry, the liveryman.' None of the marshals were impressed, at least none of them nodded. Barry was a man with small, weak eyes, a thick, coarse face, with a small mouth. He looked brutish and unintelligent. He left the impression of being a man with very high self-esteem, a bullying kind of individual whom other men would privately think very little of.

He pointed a finger at Jack Royce. 'I want that horse back, damn it. If you'd been outside doin' your business, Lefty couldn't have run off like he did.'

Cort was sympathetic. 'You might be right,' he told the ferret-eyed liveryman, and this encouraged Barry.

'Jack, damn it all, if you can't do your job we'll have to get some action from the town council, and maybe appoint us a new constable.'

Royce was gazing at Cort Lane. When Barry finished speaking the constable said, 'How long ago did he run off, Dick?'

'Half hour ago, maybe a little less—damn him.'

Royce gazed at Lane again. 'You were across the road about then. I saw you after you fired at those men skulking outside.'

Cort showed a totally innocent expression. 'I was across the road, but I wasn't inside the liverybarn when you saw me.'

Barry remembered something. 'And another thing, Jack; that confounded whelp stole my best sixgun too.'

Constable Royce went to his desk, leaned there and looked steadily at the liveryman. 'In case you didn't know it, Dick, I've got my hands full tonight. You were in the saloon a while back when I was up there, you know damned well I'm sitting atop a powder-keg. I'll do what I can about your stolen horse when I get free of this other mess.' Royce kept scowling at the ugly liveryman. 'What are they doing up the road, Dick?'

The liveryman shifted position a little, because the heat was getting through his clothing. 'I don't know,' he muttered, then he changed that as he met Cort's stare. 'Well; some of 'em has went home. Those cowboys from east of town left when the rain let up a little. Most of the townsmen left then, too.'

'How many are still up there?'

Barry thought a moment before replying. 'Ten maybe. No more'n that.' Then he got irate all over again. 'Jack, that damned horse cost me sixty dollars. He was one of my best animals. It was you talked me into hiring Lefty couple years back, because he was a good worker. I done it against my better judgement—he's a drinker and—'

'But you kept him two years,' said Cort, and went over to the door. 'Go on home, Mister Barry.' He opened the door a little, enough to allow a fresh gust of wind to rush inside, and dropped his right hand to the butt of his Colt.

The liveryman looked closely at the federal officers, then turned upon Constable Royce

145

again. 'I'm going to see the town council if you don't get that horse back within a week, Jack. You can depend on that!'

Cort closed the door after the liveryman, barred it, then made a cigarette and went to take Barry's place in front of the stove, to expedite his own drying out.

Royce stared at him. 'Deputy, if it wasn't Lefty who took you and Lige Wyatt to the edge of town, then who was it?'

Cort answered evenly. 'I've already told you. It was Lige's father. Henry Wyatt.'

Royce nodded. 'All right; and if it was Henry Wyatt, then how did he happen—?'

'Ask Lefty when you catch him,' growled Cort, before Royce could complete the question. 'Henry Wyatt bribed him. You can get all the details from Lefty. I don't know them all.' Cort turned to the cell room door, opened it and walked down to look at Jim Swain, who was standing near the rear of his cell, smoking. Swain's expression did not show much as he said, 'Whoever cut loose with that scattergun must have run clean out of the country; it's been awful quiet around here for the past half hour or so. Was that you?'

Cort shook his head. 'The town constable. Anything you need?'

Swain grinned. 'Yeah. A gun.'

Cort smiled. 'You'll have to manufacture your own.'

146

'Where's the kid?' asked Swain.

'Gone.'

That did not seem to surprise the wanted fugitive. 'This is the kind of a town a man can bust out of, if he has just a little help, Deputy. What're my chances?'

Cort shrugged. 'Got any friends in Lincoln?'

'No. Don't know a soul here.'

'Then I'd say your chances were about the same as those of a snowball in hell, Swain.'

Cort returned to the front office when Matt summoned him. 'Believe it or not,' said Matt, 'a stage just come plodding into town from the south. They'd put on an extra front-horse hitch and they was walking along like it was hard work, all six horses.'

Cort went to a window and peered out, but the coach was no longer visible up the northward roadway. Jack Royce said, 'It's the morning stage,' and that made Cort dig out his watch, flick open the face and peer at the little spidery hands. It was almost five o'clock in the morning!

The sky was still dark, the wind had died again, and it seemed that even the rainfall was falling off to a cold mist. Cort put up his watch. 'Where in hell did the time go?' he asked no one in particular. He looked out a front window again. There were still lights up at the saloon. Without turning he made a casual observation. 'The feller who did the best last night was the

147

barman.'

Al and Matt sank down upon some wall-benches, looking tired but relieved. One of them said, 'They surely won't try raiding the jailhouse now, will they, Constable?'

Royce shook his head without speaking, sank down behind his desk and held a tin cup of coffee to his lips. 'This has been the gawddamnest mess I've ever been mixed up in in my life,' he announced, and ignored the other lawmen as he tasted the coffee. 'And I got a bad feeling that it's cost me my job.' Then he turned, finally. 'But at least no one got killed, and there wasn't a hanging-bee.'

Cort turned, leaning upon the front wall, 'You did right well, Constable. Like I told you back a few hours, it's your conscience you've got to answer to, not your friends. You kept peace in your town. As for the kid . . .' Cort shrugged as someone walking heavily down from the northerly part of town called ahead in a gruff, commanding tone.

Cort hitched up the door-bar, opened the door without even looking out, and Marshal Ben Farley walked into the office bundled in a blanketcoat and wearing gloves. He flinched a little from the lamplight, gazed at the tired, slouching men, and said, 'Nothing happened, eh?'

Four sets of eyes went to Farley's face and clung there, but Jack Royce had the most

148

baleful glare as he replied.

'Yeah, something happened. It rained all night. If you want to know the rest of it, ask him.' Royce levelled a stiff finger in Cort's direction.

Farley ignored this accusing finger and stepped to the stove. The coffee-pot was empty. He raised it, shook it, then set it back down with a disgusted expression. 'I got back a reply to my telegram to Denver,' he said. 'They don't have any men to spare, so whatever's done up here, we'll have to do.'

Royce retreated into his own private silence behind the desk, but Matt and Al and Cort heeded the Marshal. Farley had a sensible suggestion. 'Let's go up to the saloon and have a drink.'

Royce's head jerked up. 'You can't go up there.'

Farley scowled. 'Why not?'

'Well; for one thing your man Lane shot a feller in the leg last night. For another thing we was just told there are still eight or ten pretty damned mad men up there. You might start a fight.'

Ben Farley thought on that a moment, stepped to the wall-rack, lifted down a sawed-off shotgun, broke it to check that both barrels were loaded, then snapped it closed and smiled benignly at Constable Royce. 'I reckon we'll make out all right. Care to come along,

Constable?'

'No!'

Farley's smile faded, his cruel, hard eyes bored into Jack Royce until the constable put down his cup and arose.

They left the jailhouse, locked it from outside, slipped and cursed their way across the road to the far plankwalk, then hiked northward. Off in the distant east a weak but steadily widening blue-grey streak firmed up. Overhead, the clouds seemed to be breaking up; stars shone, here and there, through the tattered shards of stormclouds. The rain had stopped, finally, although water still ran in rivulets, like bursted veins, out in the roadway, and every overhead rafter-end dripped.

The town was dark and sullenly silent. The only lights still showing brightly were at the saloon and down inside the long runway of the liverybarn. Otherwise, Lincoln had given up its night-long vigil.

Inside the saloon, six men who had been drinking most of the night, stood greyly along the bar, and three other men, who did not seem to be suffering so much although they had probably also had their share to drink earlier, glanced up as Constable Royce and four whisker-stubbled, rumpled, hard-looking other men, entered from the roadway. No one said a word although it was very obvious to the men in the saloon who those other four men were.

The bartender had both hands below the bar when Marshal Farley led his deputies inside. Farley swung the scattergun, with a thumb on the hammer, and the barman's hands sprang up atop his bar in plain sight. 'Just fishing for glasses in the water-bucket,' he croaked.

Farley lowered the scattergun. 'Go ahead and fish up five of them, mister, and gawddamn you, they'd better *be* glasses.'

They were. The barman asked deferentially what everyone wanted. Only Farley asked for beer, everyone else, including the town constable, ordered whisky.

The other men, part of that night-long council of lynchers, watched, and neither moved nor spoke. Cort faced away from the bar, right hand hanging relaxed, down at his side. He looked from man to man and found not one bit of real fight in any of them.

Three men, the three who looked as though they had survived the night the best, left the saloon. Those other men up along the bar, departed one at a time. When they were all gone Constable Royce raised his eyebrows at the barman, who said, 'They give it up long ago, Jack. Right after someone cut loose on 'em with a shotgun. Pardner, I never put in such a lousy night in all my life.'

Cort faced forward, lifted his glass and said, 'Amen.'

CHAPTER SEVENTEEN

RIDING WEST

When they took Jim Swain out of his cell the following morning, the sun was shining, heat was increasing, steam was rising off rooftops and from the muddy roadway, and Swain, who had not even tried to sleep until about five o'clock that morning, blinked and rubbed his eyes and cursed.

It had been Ben Farley's idea to have everyone present when he and his men departed, after committing Swain to the mercies of the Lincoln constable and Town Council. There had been some discussion up at the bar about leaving Swain in such a place, even for no longer than it would require for the Montana authorities to extradite him. Cort's opinion had been that Swain was safer in Lincoln than *he* was; Swain was no more than an outlaw, a fugitive, to the people of Lincoln, while Cort had shot one citizen and had scattered several others with gunshots. Ben Farley had agreed, at least to the extent of believing Jim Swain was safe. Constable Royce, when called upon for his judgement, had agreed with absolutely no enthusiasm, that Jim Swain was safe. When they were all in Royce's jailhouse office Ben

Farley explained to the town councilmen what he proposed; leaving Swain in their care until he was extradited. No one raised a dissenting voice, but one man, the general store proprietor, said, 'He don't mean anything to us, an' providing we don't have to feed him for six months or so, you can leave him here, Marshal, but what we want to know is just exactly what you figure to do about those Wyatts—Henry and that boy of his.'

Farley, who had talked for an hour with Cort about the Wyatts, said, 'They are on our wanted list. Being federal fugitives doesn't work much in a man's favour, mister.'

The store-keeper was not satisfied. 'Maybe not, but this town's got reason to want the Wyatts arrested and imprisoned.'

Farley gazed thoughtfully at his interrogator. 'All right. Tell us where they are and we'll go after them.'

The store-keeper scowled. 'How would I know where they are?'

Farley had an answer to that. It was the same reply he'd been giving people who aggravated him for a long time. 'Then don't ask us to perform miracles. We're not a damn bit smarter than you are—in fact, because we put our lives on the line almost every day to protect people like you, maybe we're dumber. Anyone can criticize, mister, so unless you can come up with something constructive, leave our business to us. We do passably well at it.'

That ended the town council's part of the meeting in Jack Royce's office. The councilmen filed out, irritated, no doubt, but unable to crack through Ben Farley's obduracy. Jim Swain had listened, and was softly smiling as Farley turned towards him and said, 'With any luck they'll send down from Montana for you within a week or so. They're building a new prison up at Deer Lodge. You might get in on helping to fell the trees and build the place. As far as we're concerned, you're no longer our headache.'

Swain shrugged and made a cigarette. As he lit up he said, 'Marshal; the kid's no outlaw. I don't know about his paw; don't know that much about him, but the kid don't even have what it takes to make an outlaw. As for me—I'll look after myself. I've been doing that for a lot of years.'

Swain went over to the cell room door and waited for Jack Royce to walk over, lead him back to his cell and lock him in. While those two were out of the room Marshal Farley said, 'Cort, which way did you say the Wyatts rode when they quit town last night?'

'Northward.'

Farley pondered that a moment. 'Odd thing; you know, when I was coming up from the south real early this morning in the rain, I saw a couple of riders heading southward. One of them was wearing a black raincoat and the other was tall and skinny, like that lad was.'

Al took it up. 'Must have been two other fellers, Ben. Matt and I saw the Wyatts heading north, too.'

Matt soberly nodded his head. 'And they was *both* wearing long black slickers, not just one of them. You must have seen a couple of other men, Marshal.'

Ben Farley look from man to man, then muttered his response to this unanimous lying. 'Must have been two other fellers. But you know, I wondered when I saw them, what in hell would make a couple of fellers ride on a night like that was. It'd have to be pretty damned important.'

Cort went to the door, glanced across at the liverybarn and when Ben Farley spoke to him, Cort said, 'We'd better get saddled up and on the road, Marshal.'

They were leaving the jailhouse when Constable Royce returned from locking Swain into his cell. Royce trooped along in the wake of the federal officers. Out front of the liverybarn that brutish-faced liveryman, Richard Barry, met them with a bullying, hostile expression. No one spoke to him nor even nodded, which left Barry standing there. Five armed men, four of them perfectly willing to tangle with him, stirred in the liveryman's tight, unintelligent little brain an instinctive urging towards

155

wariness. He only glared harder at Jack Royce, then he went walking up in the direction of the general store, which left the saddling and bridling to his day-man, and to the federal officers.

Royce helped, silently. When it was all done and Marshal Farley's men were mounted and ready to depart, Royce said, 'I'm not sorry to see you boys leave and I hope to hell you don't come back . . . But if there's any serious trouble around here again, I may send for you.'

Cort smiled at this honest expression of feeling. He and the others nodded to Royce and rode out into the roadway, turned southward, and under the watchful eyes of two-thirds of the town of Lincoln, they rode to the far end of town, then turned off towards the west, and as soon as they had solid footing upon the rangeland, they loped their rested horses for a mile, or until Lincoln was hull-down on the rearward horizon, then they hauled down to a walk.

Ben Farley gazed northwards, up where the landforms changed, where the uplands lay, beyond a series of serrated, tree-speckled, upended little foothills. 'They went north, did they?' he mused aloud. The other men exchanged guarded looks, then solemnly confirmed that the Wyatts had, indeed, ridden northward. Farley looped his reins, fished inside his blanketcoat, brought forth four cigars, passed them around, and after lighting his own cigar, he said, 'Wasn't any warrant on them, and no one back in Lincoln signed a complaint—which I was afraid someone might remember to do before we got out of there—so the hell with it.' He removed his cigar and looked at it. 'There aren't too many things a man can find in towns that add much to living, but these here cigars sure are one of them.'

Cort, Al and Matt relaxed. They knew Ben Farley well enough to realize he had just said all he would ever say about the kid, and the kid's father, which suited them right down to the ground. They were manhunting-lawmen, not wet-nurses.

Photoset, printed and bound in Great Britain by REDWOOD BURN LIMITED, Trowbridge, Wiltshire

m